P9-DOC-361

"Addi?"

Addison's heart twisted. She knew that voice, and only one man had ever called her by that nickname. Drew Bryant, her long-dead fiancé.

She shook her head. Clearly she'd let the stress and worry get to her. Drew wasn't here, wasn't even alive.

The screen door hinges squealed and the handle of the main door turned. A dream, she thought, it had to be a dream. As the door eased open, Addison leveled the shotgun at the man casting shadows across the weak moonlight spilling through the door.

"Addi, it's me, Drew. I'm here to help."

Addison fired.

The loud report deafened her to the splintering wood as the buckshot pelted the front door. The man rushed forward, taking the gun before she could fire again.

"It's *me*," he said, his voice lost in the ringing in her ears.

The single lightbulb came on and she covered her mouth, barely smothering the scream lodged in her chest. "No. *No.*" This wasn't possible.

TO HONOR AND TO PROTECT

USA TODAY Bestselling Authors

DEBRA WEBB
& REGAN BLACK

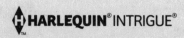
HARLEQUIN® INTRIGUE®

If you purchased this book without a cover you should be aware
that this book is stolen property. It was reported as "unsold and
destroyed" to the publisher, and neither the author nor the
publisher has received any payment for this "stripped book."

For Robert, if you never read past this page,
know that you're my treasure, full of the integrity,
insight and kindness that make real-life heroes so special.

ISBN-13: 978-0-373-74890-7

To Honor and To Protect

Copyright © 2015 by Debra Webb

Recycling programs
for this product may
not exist in your area.

All rights reserved. Except for use in any review, the reproduction or
utilization of this work in whole or in part in any form by any electronic,
mechanical or other means, now known or hereinafter invented, including
xerography, photocopying and recording, or in any information storage
or retrieval system, is forbidden without the written permission of the
publisher, Harlequin Enterprises Limited, 225 Duncan Mill Road,
Don Mills, Ontario M3B 3K9, Canada.

This is a work of fiction. Names, characters, places and incidents are
either the product of the author's imagination or are used fictitiously,
and any resemblance to actual persons, living or dead, business
establishments, events or locales is entirely coincidental.

This edition published by arrangement with Harlequin Books S.A.

For questions and comments about the quality of this book,
please contact us at CustomerService@Harlequin.com.

® and TM are trademarks of Harlequin Enterprises Limited or its
corporate affiliates. Trademarks indicated with ® are registered in the
United States Patent and Trademark Office, the Canadian Intellectual
Property Office and in other countries.

Printed in U.S.A.

Debra Webb, born in Alabama, wrote her first story at age nine and her first romance at thirteen. It wasn't until she spent three years working for the military behind the Iron Curtain—and a five-year stint with NASA—that she realized her true calling. Since then the *USA TODAY* bestselling author has penned more than one hundred novels, including her internationally bestselling Colby Agency series.

Regan Black, a *USA TODAY* bestselling author, writes award-winning, action-packed novels featuring kick-butt heroines and the sexy heroes who fall in love with them. Raised in the Midwest and California, she and her family, along with their adopted greyhound, two arrogant cats and a quirky finch, reside in the South Carolina Lowcountry, where the rich blend of legend, romance and history fuels her imagination.

Books by Debra Webb and Regan Black

HARLEQUIN INTRIGUE

The Specialists: Heroes Next Door series

The Hunk Next Door
Heart of a Hero
To Honor and To Protect

Visit the Author Profile page at
Harlequin.com for more titles.

CAST OF CHARACTERS

***Addison (Addi) Collins*—**One of San Francisco's top corporate attorneys and a single mom, Addison is still searching for success in her personal life. Her first fiancé was killed in a military operation, and her new fiancé might be a dangerous traitor.

***Drew Bryant*—**As a Special Forces soldier, Drew's wedding was interrupted by a mission that ended with his capture and nearly two years as a prisoner of war in the Middle East. Having escaped, he's back in the States trying to pick up the pieces of his life.

***Thomas Casey*—**The director of the Specialists has been ordered to find and plug an intelligence leak that has compromised covert operatives and missions around the world.

***Craig Everett*—**A successful San Francisco businessman, he made his fortune advising global investors, but he could lose everything if his fiancée exposes his secret connections.

Chapter One

Interstate 10, West Texas
Thursday, June 19, 3:10 p.m.

Addison Collins checked the fuel gauge, quickly calculating how many more miles she could put between her and the inevitable pursuit before they had to stop. Her brand-new BMW could've done that for her, but not this ancient, new-to-her Land Rover. That was what math was for, wasn't it? This was the perfect example she would keep in the back of her mind for the day her son complained about his math homework.

"Mom, how much longer?"

She recognized that tone. He was about to complain but not about math. Using the rearview mirror, she aimed a confident smile at her son. His bright hair gleamed in the sunlight coming through the window, but the glare on his face bordered on mutinous.

She couldn't blame him. They'd been on the

road for two days straight and had another day left. Possibly more. "About another half hour and we'll stop again."

"I have to pee now."

"You'll have to hold it for a few minutes."

"A half hour is *thirty* minutes. A few is more like three."

Instead of maternal pride, Addison couldn't help wondering why she'd ever been inclined to teach him the difference. "And how many threes are in thirty?"

"Ten." He turned his face to the window. "I still have to pee."

"All right. I'll find a place to stop."

"This car stinks," he said a minute later.

"The car is clean. It's just new-car smell." With a persistent undertone of mildew, but she kept that thought to herself.

"But it's an *old* car."

"True." *Patience will pay off.* "The car dealers spray a strong deodorizer to make it feel new." They had periodically rolled down the windows, but the heavy-duty deodorizer scent lingered, punctuating the mildew rather than overpowering it. This vehicle might be a major step down in value from her BMW, but the dealer in Arizona had been willing to meet her trade and cash terms without any questions, and that had been priceless.

"Why?"

"So they can sell it faster."

"Will our car stink like this when we go back home?"

"I don't know." It was the only safe answer because she hadn't yet found the courage to tell her son they weren't going back. She hadn't lied to him and she wouldn't start now, but she wasn't ready to discuss it. The words he needed to hear to understand the gravity of their new situation just weren't coming to her, and she wasn't ready to cope with the fallout when he realized he wouldn't see his friends again.

Her own grief was too fresh, her fear of the unknown too big. When she had a handle on her feelings, she would be better able to help him with his. *Coward*, an annoying little voice in her head muttered.

"It's yucky in here," he said, making a gagging noise. He had a point, though she wasn't about to admit it. "I feel sick."

Addison's patience was fraying, but it wasn't Andy's fault they were in this mess. No, this was all her doing. She'd been the one to screw up their picture-perfect life by getting conned by a not-nearly perfect man. He'd looked like Mr. Right, and until a few days ago, she'd been sure he was the right man for both her and Andy. The only silver lining—and she was clinging to it—was that she'd learned the truth before the wedding.

"Roll down the window," she said. "Some fresh air should help."

His face brightened momentarily, then clouded over again. "Where's the button?"

She rolled her eyes. "Use that little handle thingy."

"Huh?"

She stretched but couldn't reach it from the driver's seat. The Land Rover was built so much wider than her sedan, and the only power was under the hood. How ridiculous that an old-school vehicle could stump them both. "The window isn't electric like you're used to. Just wind it down, remember?"

She had a few minutes of peace while the manual crank amused her seven-year-old son. In a few months, he'd be eight. Although less than a week ago she'd been kicking around ideas for his birthday party, now all bets were off. She didn't know where they'd be living by his birthday, only that she intended to be sure they were both alive to celebrate it—even if it was just the two of them.

She immediately pushed that train of thought off the tracks. Right now all Andy needed to know was that they were on a summer adventure. Providing for him, taking care of his education—those questions would be answered later.

"Are we there yet?"

Not even close. "Almost."

"Mom, I can't hold it much longer."

"Hang on." With her eyes on the road, she caught the squirming in the backseat. "There's a place at this next exit."

"How long?"

"Two minutes," she replied, her voice leaving no room for argument. "You can time me."

His small, straight nose wrinkled as he fiddled with the big Captain America watch on his wrist. He flipped up the red, white and blue shield cover and busied himself with the stopwatch feature. Her little man had begged for the watch for Christmas and had worn it from the moment he'd ripped open the package. Only his fear of ruining it made him take it off for bath time.

She happily nurtured his love of comic book heroes, and reading through various adventures with him was part of their bedtime routine. Even in the horrible, desperate rush to get away, she'd grabbed his entire collection. More than once she'd wondered if some part of his attraction to comics was genetic. Andy's father had been a soldier, a good man and a lifelong fan of the Marvel universe. Oh, what she wouldn't give to have him here with her now.

"One minute," Andy announced.

"My personal town crier," she mumbled, taking the exit.

"What's a town crier?"

Nothing wrong with her boy's hearing. "Lots and lots of years ago, people didn't have smartphones or clocks or watches, so someone would walk the town streets and call out the time. 'Three o'clock and all's well!' Like that."

"Huh."

"We're here." She pulled into the parking space closest to the front door of the gas station, knowing that thoughtful "huh" sound meant more questions were dancing at the front of his brain. "You can unbuckle now."

"You made it with ten seconds to spare."

"Guess I should've been a race car driver."

"Did town criers drive this old kind of car?" he asked when she came around to open his door.

"No. Town criers were way before cars."

"Then how did they get around town?"

She held out her hand, her heart giving a happy bump when he placed his in hers without argument. "People walked or used horses and carts."

"That's weird. Horses poop a lot."

She laughed. "Everything has a by-product." Inside, she glanced around for the restroom sign, leading her son back by way of the motor oil aisle rather than the candy aisle. "I know at school you've seen pictures of cities before cars."

"And the museum field trips." He shrugged, his gaze roving across the labels at his eye level, his feet slowing as he tried to read the words and logos on each one. Grateful for the distraction, she wasn't surprised it didn't last. When she pushed open the ladies' room door, he stopped short in the narrow hallway.

"I'm a boy," he whispered as if she might've forgotten.

"Road rules, remember? We stick together."

"Mom." He scowled at her and folded his arms across his chest. "I'm too old to go in there."

She bent close to his ear. "I understand. I even almost agree."

"Almost?" He tilted his head, wary.

She nodded, smothering the smile for the sake of his pride. "But today it's a safety issue. We stay together."

"It's been nothin' but safety since we left home."

"I know. And it has to be safety for a little longer." She silently vowed to make it up to him. Somehow. "Soon you'll have all kinds of new places and things to discover on our adventure."

"Promise?"

"Yes."

He looked back at her with the big, soft brown eyes that reminded her more and more of his father. His small hand patted her cheek. "If it makes you feel better, I'll stay with you."

"Thank you."

"But I want to make a new deal for when I turn eight."

"That's certainly up for discussion." Right now she had to be sure they lived that long.

With bladders relieved and hands washed thoroughly to the tune of the alphabet song, they cut through the store to get back on the road.

"Can I have a Coke?"

"It's 'may I,'" she corrected automatically. "And no. We have water in the car."

"Can I have a peanut butter cup?"

So much for her efforts to avoid the candy and junk food. "When we stop for dinner tonight, you can have a Coke and a peanut butter cup."

"Both?" His eyes went wide with hope.

She nodded.

"How long to dinner?"

She laughed and checked her watch. "A few hours." She wanted more distance between her and the man who had the resources to chase her off the edge of the world. Addison refused to think of him as her fiancé anymore. Although she'd done her best to blur any trail, to escape somewhere he didn't even know to search, she couldn't be sure it would work.

The idea of being so completely duped by Craig Everett infuriated her. Worse, her relationship with him was now an embarrassment in both the professional and personal context. When she thought of how much she'd shared with that worthless excuse for a man, she wanted to shoot something. Preferably Craig. They'd shared lovely romantic evenings, family-type outings with Andy and lazy sleep-late weekend mornings. All of it made her feel dirty now.

Assuming she could evade Craig until she got word the authorities had him locked down, assuming she could eventually return to her life in San Francisco, she wasn't quite sure how she'd find the courage to look her friends or her boss in the eye again.

It was hopeless to think his arrest and illegal dealings wouldn't make news up and down the West Coast. More likely, it would be national news for a short time. Which meant she and Andy would be dragged into Craig's horrendous mess by association. Their lives would be picked apart and exposed for everyone in the world to judge. It was possible even her secluded destination in the uncharted depths of a Louisiana swamp wouldn't be shelter enough.

Because she'd been the idiot who nearly married an American traitor.

She buckled Andy into the booster seat and closed the door, stifling the violent words that wanted to pour out of her whenever she thought about what Craig had done. Telling herself she'd broken up his system and stopped him didn't help as much as it should. Maybe that would change with time. So many things did.

The facts crawled like a line of ants between her shoulder blades. The sensation grew worse when she considered the likelihood that Craig's slimy dealings had cost other women—other families—the grief she'd felt when Andy's father had been killed in action on the other side of the world.

If Drew Bryant, her favorite soldier, were alive he'd…

Biting her lip, she pulled herself together. If Drew were alive, all of this would be irrelevant. Unnecessary. She, Drew and Andy would be a family, settled in some happy suburb or on farmland far from California. A road trip like this really would be a grand summer adventure. Complete with two drivers and possibly a brother or sister in the backseat with Andy. Even when she and Drew were children themselves, they'd dreamed of having a big family.

If Drew were alive, she wouldn't have been with Craig at all. It would've been up to someone else to catch that traitorous, double-talking jerk trading secrets and sensitive military information with who knew how many unsavory people.

If, if, if. Exasperated with herself, Addison slid into the driver's seat and moved the car to the gas pump. Might as well top it off while she was here. Hopefully it would save her a stop later.

No matter how she coached herself, she wasn't sure catching Craig qualified as a blessing in disguise, not when she knew it could cost her everything she held dear. But turning over the information she'd found had been automatic, a reflex she couldn't suppress any more than breathing. No one should profit from the pain and suffering of others.

Craig had made a fortune for himself and others through legal means. Discovering the fortune he'd amassed through illegal negotiations had shocked her. She couldn't fathom how he'd made that leap into predatory dealings. She'd only scraped the tip of the iceberg, but she knew without any doubt what would happen if Craig or his nasty colleagues caught up with her and Andy before the authorities took action.

She smiled at her son through the window as she pumped gas. Being the whistle-blower was difficult for anyone, but a single mom? Although she couldn't abide letting Craig go unpunished, she kept wondering if there'd been a better way to take him down. She'd completely altered two lives when she'd sent the files as an anonymous tip to the local FBI office. All she could do now was hide and pray for the best.

A few more miles down the road Andy piped up again. "Are we going to SeaWorld?"

She'd noticed the billboard, too, and the question wasn't unreasonable, but she found herself wishing for nightfall. "Not this trip, honey." Thinking of the crowds and security cameras raised goose bumps along her arms. An attraction like that could prove more risk than entertainment.

"Will Craig have part of our summer adventure with us?"

Only in my nightmares, she thought. "Not this trip," she repeated, glancing at the elaborate engagement ring that remained on her hand. Taking it off would have Andy asking still more questions she wasn't ready to answer. Once they reached the bayou she'd throw the damn thing to the nearest alligator. Imagining Craig's outrage over that move made her smile.

The diamond caught the waning sunlight and she wondered—again—which part of Craig's income had paid for it. Knowing wouldn't change how she felt about wearing it, but the aching, wounded part of her heart wanted the answer. She shut that down. There was no sense in being sentimental over a man who'd not only played her for a fool, but also traded lives for money with dangerous people. People who'd want to punish her for blowing up their system. People who were probably searching for her right now. Maybe it would be smart to sell the gaudy thing. She could invest the proceeds for Andy's college fund. That seemed like a fair enough solution.

"I miss him already," Andy murmured from the backseat.

"I know." Craig was the closest thing Andy had had to a father figure because his father had died before he was born. It made her cringe now, in light of his treacherous side business, but it would be another point of grief for her son when he learned that relationship was over. Forever.

Of all the challenges ahead of her, she dreaded navigating that particular tightrope. How could she ever adequately explain her choices to a seven-year-old who'd been so eager for a dad? In Andy's eyes, Craig had reached near-hero status. Now, thanks to her, in Craig's eyes she and her son were no more than risks to eliminate. That was more truth than Andy needed weighing on his young shoulders.

"Will the whole adventure be in this old car?"

"No." She'd hesitated to tell him where they were going, fearful that someone would overhear his chatter during a stop. "Do you think you'd like SeaWorld?"

"Yes! They have whales and dolphins and sharks and turtles and you can swim with them."

"That does sound like fun."

"Please can we go, Mom?"

"I can't make promises, but if it's possible, yes, we'll go to SeaWorld." Eventually.

"Cool! Jeff and Caleb will be jealous. We'll take lots of pictures, right?"

"Of course." As long as those pictures wouldn't jeopardize their secrets.

"I want to pet a shark."

You've already been too close, she thought, checking her rearview mirror. *We just didn't see his teeth.* Yet.

"We'll see."

"That means no."

"Not in our house," she said with more bite than she'd intended. "We've talked about that. I need to concentrate right now, okay?"

"Okay."

"We'll stop for dinner in two hours." She smiled, determined to regain her composure. "Can you set an alarm, please?"

"Sure!"

"Thank you." She checked her mirrors and stared at the long ribbon of highway cluttered with traffic. Once she saw Andy was focused on his handheld game, she turned on the radio, hoping to catch some announcement of Craig's situation. She wouldn't feel safe until he was in custody, and she wouldn't come out of hiding until she was sure his connections had been found. But she heard no updates.

Hours later, when Addison and Andy stopped for dinner, she ducked into a post office for one last precaution. An insurance policy of sorts, in case Craig found a loophole. Letting Andy push the buttons on the automated kiosk machine in the lobby, she breathed a little better when he sent the envelope into the chute.

Whatever happened next, now she could be sure someone else knew the truth about Craig and his involvement in her life.

"Are you mad?" Andy asked, taking her hand as they returned to the car.

"Not with you." She was definitely mad, but more than the anger, she felt a consuming, unfamiliar terror. All her life she'd known what to do and when to do it. There had been nerves and mistakes, sadness and joy along the way, but overall, she'd had a dream, created a plan and worked tirelessly to make it all a reality for her and her son.

"Then who're you mad at?"

She considered her answer as he boosted himself back up into the car. "Myself," she replied honestly. "I made a big mistake."

"Is that why we're on this summer adventure?"

Occasionally her son was too perceptive for

her comfort. "Partly," she said with a smile. "But summer is the perfect time for a big adventure."

"We won't be in the car the whole time, will we?"

"Already asked and answered, young man," she said with a laugh. "I promise the real adventure will begin soon." She thought of the frogs and birds, the still, reflective black water and tall cypress trees where they were headed. He would love it all, so different from any camp or field trip he'd experienced. "You're going to have all kinds of fun."

"Promise?"

"Have I ever let you down?"

He actually gave it some thought before he replied, "No."

"Well, I don't plan to start now."

His grin, full of eagerness and love, was too reminiscent of his father. It had her heart aching for what might have been as they got back on the road. Since losing Drew before Andy's birth, she'd made a practice of focusing on the present. Of course she'd told her son bits and pieces about his real dad as he'd been able to understand them, but with no living relatives in the Bryant family, it seemed best for both of them not to dwell on what couldn't be changed.

Long after the dinner stop, as she crossed the state line into Louisiana, the news hit the radio.

Federal authorities had arrested Craig at his posh home in San Francisco. Addison didn't breathe easy until the reporter finished the explanation with no mention of her name.

Understanding what he'd done, the scope of his crimes and that the FBI probably already knew she'd turned him in, she knew her anonymity wouldn't last long, but she intended to make the most of her temporary advantage.

Chapter Two

Washington, DC
Wednesday, July 2, 9:15 a.m.

Andrew "Drew" Bryant remained in his seat, his back straight, palms relaxed on his thighs, gaze straight ahead. Maintaining a calm facade in all circumstances had been emphasized during his time with the Special Forces, but he'd mastered the skill as a prisoner of war. He'd memorized and evaluated every detail of his surroundings. The sleek, understated decor of the lobby, the expensive black leather seating and the polished chrome and glass accents might be found in any number of office buildings around the world, but the distinct lack of nameplates and office logos on the doors told him more than anyone behind those doors wanted him to know. At one time in his life he might've paced the marble-floored lobby impatiently, but not anymore. These days, he let the world come to him.

He was more than a little relieved the men in dark suits who'd picked him up twelve hours ago hadn't put a bag over his head. It could still happen, and if it did, it would test his fitful control. He took a deep breath. Calm was key. In every situation. No sense proving the army docs right about his uncertain mental state.

They'd left him alone and unrestrained, but he'd seen the escort lock the elevator. If they wanted him to sit here, here was where he'd sit. He was in a high-rent office building, but the view from the window wasn't helpful, with no visible skyline beyond tall trees. The artwork on the walls and in the elevator was most likely original. In his assessment, that meant this place didn't get a lot of foot traffic.

Drew felt his heart rate tick up as another minute passed. He couldn't help recalling the last time he'd been snatched away from a normal day. Except that day hadn't been normal at all. It had been his wedding day.

On that occasion he'd been ordered to duty in the middle of the night and it had required half a pot of coffee to burn away the fuzzy aftertaste of his bachelor party. He'd left a note—unauthorized but nonnegotiable—for his bride. The woman who'd eventually given up on him. Not that he blamed her.

He kept his eyes forward, even as the sound

of feminine high heels clicked across the marble floor on the other side of the door. Closer, closer, then fading away.

Had his bride chosen heels or flats? He recalled overhearing the debate with her maid of honor, but he'd never known the final decision.

The last time he'd been uprooted on the precipice of a major life event his commanding officer had insisted there'd been no time for even a cursory marriage ceremony. This time, someone with serious money and authority had pulled him away from a major basketball game between the top two teams in the Detroit recreational league. The score tied, less than five minutes left, he'd been forced away. Unable to stem the curiosity, Drew gave in and glanced at his watch. The game had ended hours ago and without his phone, he still didn't know who won.

It pissed him off. Bragging rights were riding on that game, and these days that was all the stress he wanted, but life rarely cooperated with his wants.

Drew snorted as another minute clicked by on the wall clock. The kids he worked with in Detroit kept him from wallowing in self-pity after the army had shown him the door with an early retirement for medical reasons. Retired at thirty-six years old. Unbelievable. That hadn't been part of the plan. He rarely let it bother him, but today when something from his past was clearly interrupting his present, he couldn't shake off the irritation.

He knew this drill, knew someone from the alphabet soup of government agencies had pulled strings to drag him out of Detroit last night. But if it was so important it couldn't wait until the end of the game, why was he parked in limbo here?

The high heels approached once more and Drew shifted his face, his entire body into neutral. The heels stopped and the glass door opened with an understated *whoosh*.

"Mr. Bryant?"

"Yes." He stood, facing the woman who remained in the doorway. She was slender, her sleek navy blue dress making a professional and feminine statement. Noting the long legs and high heels, he pegged her as a dancer by training. Watching her approach, he knew she was an expert in martial arts, as well. If a woman like this was merely a receptionist in this place, he might be in more trouble than he could handle.

"Our apologies for the delay," she said with a polite smile. "I've been told you might appreciate this video while you wait. It shouldn't be much longer." She handed him a tablet and returned to her side of the glass doors.

He looked at the screen, baffled as he recognized the basketball court and uniforms of the players. It couldn't be… He sank back into his chair and, touching the icon, put the video into motion. "I'll be damned," he muttered, watching the last minutes of the basketball game.

Immersed in the video action, he forgot where he was, forgot to wonder why, and just enjoyed watching his team take the win in a nail-biting last-second shot. "Yes!" He pumped his fist and watched as one of the more headstrong kids from the neighborhood enjoyed a hero's celebration.

Drew took a deep breath, relieved and relaxed that his kids were making progress within the community. Something was finally going right. That neighborhood, those kids were coming together as a team and as a family of sorts. Knowing his small part in the overall puzzle made a difference was enough to keep him moving forward instead of stalling out.

A big accomplishment for a man who'd nearly lost his mind when the life he'd dreamed of slipped out of his grasp. *Stolen* was a more accurate term, but according to the army shrinks, that word held negative connotations. They wanted him to reframe, rephrase, re-everything when all he wanted was to rewind and make a different choice in the early hours of his wedding day.

"They're ready for you now, Mr. Bryant."

She was back and he hadn't even heard her approach. He knew better, knew he had to keep his mind off the past or it would swallow him up. Drew stood and smiled. "Thanks for this." He extended the tablet.

"You're welcome." She accepted the device with another courteous smile. "This way."

He followed the slender woman, the only sound the click of her heels, but even that went quiet when she turned down a carpeted hallway. They passed a bank of blacked-out windows of what was probably a conference room. When they passed another small reception area and one nearly closed office door, Drew's stomach dropped.

They were headed for the corner office, a destination that in his experience didn't ever add up to anything good. The woman stopped at the open door, announced him, then stepped back. Going forward was the only option. She closed the door behind him as he entered.

He felt underdressed in his gym clothes compared to the man in the dark suit and expensive tie. The man rose from his elegant chair and came around the desk quickly, hand extended. "I'm Director Thomas Casey." The grip was firm and brief as they shook hands. "Come have a seat, Mr. Bryant."

Drew couldn't hide his surprise. Thomas Casey was one of those names whispered in dark corners by people with the highest clearances.

Among the microcommunity of black ops and special operations, the man who supposedly coordinated a crack team of "Specialists" was nearly urban legend. "I thought you were a myth," Drew admitted as Thomas returned to his big chair behind the desk.

"That's the way I like it." The smile was as firm and as brief as the handshake. "I appreciate your cooperation on such short notice."

"Didn't feel like there was much choice, sir."

"Call me Thomas."

Another surprise. "Sure."

"You saw the end of the game, I trust."

"Yes, thank you." He wondered if Thomas arranged for the game to be recorded, or if one of his Specialists had pulled it off YouTube.

"It came down to the wire."

Drew nodded. "Always better for both teams that way."

"Probably so." Thomas studied Drew another moment. "Solid effort and a close call incite more determination to win the next game. We understand that here," he said. "I've looked into your background as well as your present situation. What you're doing in Detroit is good work."

"I like it," Drew said, hiding his surprise at the compliment. "And I'd like to get back to it."

"I'm sure. Let's talk about that. It's not my practice to pull people away from good work, but

I find myself in a tight spot. I believe your skills and knowledge would be helpful."

Drew waited in silence, curious. He no longer had the security clearance to even sit in this room. Thomas, having poked through his background, knew that. None of Drew's kids were into anything that would be of interest to the director. He couldn't think of a single way he could be helpful, but he'd listen. It would be rude not to after he'd been hauled out here.

"You aren't curious?" Thomas asked.

"I am." But he wasn't going to reveal anything to this master spook by asking questions.

"All right." Thomas gave a wry chuckle when Drew didn't elaborate. "Federal authorities made an arrest based on an almost anonymous tip."

Almost anonymous? Drew hadn't heard that phrase before.

"The person who shared the information requested that she be left out of it and we're doing our best to honor that from an investigative standpoint."

Drew wanted to stop Thomas right there, to point out that he wasn't in the market for a bodyguard gig, didn't have the head for it anymore, but he kept his mouth shut and his ears open.

"You've been through some hard times, Mr. Bryant."

"Drew is fine," he replied, wondering why the

subject had changed. If this had something to do with the bastards who'd held him as a POW for six years in a cave in Afghanistan, he might opt in to whatever the director had in mind. A little revenge could go a long way toward healing. It was a dangerous line of thought, but Drew let it play out. Thinking about something and acting on it were two different animals. He'd learned that quickly as a prisoner and in the agonizing months of recovery that followed his escape and rescue.

"Do you feel you're fit for service?"

Drew met Thomas's assessing gaze. "Depends on the type of service, I suppose. The army found me to be more hindrance than help."

"Are you?"

"Didn't have the chance to find out," Drew blurted before thinking through a better reply.

"Tell me about your recovery."

Drew could see no way of avoiding the topic. Not in this room. Better to lay it out there than allow Thomas to continue to entertain his delusions. If the man managed to maintain myth status in a place like Washington, Drew could safely assume his personal secrets wouldn't leave the room.

Still, he played it close. "Long. Physically, I'd lost muscle mass to the malnutrition and poor conditions. That came back quick enough after a few weeks in the hospital with proper nutrition and a few months of physical therapy. They had to reset an arm and do a little work on my back."

He still felt guilty and selfish when he thought of those endless days with no contact beyond hospital staff and the occasional visit from a chaplain or army officials. He should have been full of gratitude, but instead he'd battled a terrible sense of loss and isolation no matter how they praised him for surviving.

"I heard your father died while you were a prisoner."

"Yes." His superiors had explained valid reasons for not publicizing his return to anyone, not even family. "They showed me the obituary, told me he was buried next to my mom."

"No one from your past knows you're alive. There's no reason to keep your survival a secret now."

"There's no reason to throw a parade, either," Drew countered. "A few people from my old neighborhood recognized me when I came back."

"I'm sure they were happy to see you."

"Pretty much." Almost a year later, he was okay with his neighbors, too. With his father dead, the only other person Drew had wanted to see was the bride he'd left waiting at the altar. She was the final piece of his recovery, and everyone who'd had a hand in it knew he needed to reach out to her. Too bad no one had warned him what he'd find.

Despite the years, having heard about his wedding plans from his father, the neighbors were eager to meet the woman they'd only seen in wedding announcement photos. When he'd felt strong enough, he'd gone looking for her and returned alone. After about six months his neighbors stopped asking about her.

"Took a while to get past all the sympathy," Drew said. It was all the explanation he felt Thomas needed on his personal life.

"That's reasonable."

It sure hadn't felt that way at the time, but it was done now and he had carved out a new place for himself. He might spend his nights alone, but based on the persistent nightmares, that was for the best.

The back of his neck prickling, Drew wanted to shift the topic back to Thomas's invasion of his new life, but again he waited quietly for the director to make the move.

"Addison Collins." Thomas tossed out the name, like a bomb in the middle of his desk, and leaned back to watch Drew's reaction.

His body went cold at the sound of her name. Suddenly he wanted to talk about the POW camp. The injuries. The nightmares. The dirt cell and lousy food. Anything but *her*.

"Have you had any contact with your fiancée lately?"

"Former fiancée," Drew corrected. "And no." He didn't even let himself think of her. Not after he'd seen her playing freeze tag with another man and a little boy in San Francisco last fall. He'd been close enough to see the smile on her face, to hear her carefree, happy laughter. Close enough to see the ring on her finger sporting a diamond easily twice the size of the one he'd given her years ago. She'd been so obviously settled and content with her family that he'd walked away rather than ruin her day and twist up her life.

"Why do you ask?" He ignored the calculating gleam in Thomas's quick smile. Drew could no more hold back that question than stop the next sunrise. With a nearly audible snap, a piece clicked into place. "She's the tipster."

"Yes. And she's gone missing."

"So ask her husband." Drew's throat went dry and his palms went damp. Addi was fine. Had to be fine. He couldn't accept anything else where she was concerned.

"Well…" Thomas hesitated. "You haven't seen any of the news coverage on this?"

Drew shook his head. Knowing his emotional limits, he didn't do any more than scan the local headlines, and sometimes that was more bad news than he could handle.

"Craig Everett." Thomas opened a file and showed him a picture of the man who'd been with Addi in the park. "He and Ms. Collins planned to marry at the end of the summer, but he's also gone missing."

Planned? "She's not married?" Had he missed an important chance to be with her? It was hard to think about that. He'd been so sure about what he'd seen. Maybe she'd been married and divorced before Everett came along.

"No marriage on record," Thomas confirmed. "What we do know is that she turned over damning evidence and abruptly left town. She hasn't been seen anywhere in just over two weeks."

It didn't make sense. Drew thought of the little boy, wondering if the kid belonged to Addison or Everett.

"The evidence Addison provided against Everett is excellent, but I think she knows more."

"If the evidence is so great, why do you need more?"

Thomas sighed. "Because I was informed last night that Everett escaped during a transfer between facilities."

Drew swore, unable to sit still any longer. He shifted in the chair, pushed a hand through his hair. "How'd you let that happen?"

"*I* didn't." The director's voice went cold. "Reviewing everything we have, I've concluded Everett's connections are too good. I believe Addison can confirm my suspicions and help me plug what must be a leak on the government side."

Better and better, Drew thought, but he couldn't get the image of Addison, scared and on the run, out of his mind. "What did Everett do?"

"Based on this initial evidence, he's used his contacts among import-export businesses to start a sideline brokering deals for controlled software and hard intel on human assets in sensitive areas. We're not yet sure if it started as his idea or—"

"She had nothing to do with that."

"You sound sure."

"I am." No matter how she'd moved on with her life, Addison wasn't a traitor. He could only imagine how angry she'd been to discover the secrets this Everett guy had been hiding.

"For the record, I agree with you."

No surprise. Thomas would've done all the background research on everyone involved in what must be a fiasco from the government side. It wouldn't take much legwork to look at Addison's background and find her first near-miss marriage. He clenched his fist. Her fiancé would've heard all about her past without the hassle of gathering intel. "Why am I here?"

"As I said, she's gone missing, and I think you're just the man to find her."

Would his past never stay buried? "I don't know anything about her anymore."

"Which is precisely the kind of advantage I'm looking for. No one on my team has found a trace of her since her BMW wound up in a used car lot in Arizona."

Just because she'd been south and east of San Francisco didn't mean she'd keep going that direction. "That leaves a lot of territory to cover. What about Everett?"

Thomas's expression clouded over. "Also off the radar right now. He could very well be searching for Ms. Collins, too, planning to buy her off or to silence her."

Drew understood which option was more likely. Addison had integrity in spades.

"My hope," Thomas continued, "is that you can find her first and bring her in. I can protect her."

Drew felt a hot lick of panic. This couldn't be happening. "What do you expect me to do? What do I tell her?" He'd seen the fallen hero obituary in the scrapbook his father had created. He'd read the few letters Addison had written to his dad in the months following their interrupted wedding and his capture. "She thinks I'm dead."

"I understand this is overwhelming," Thomas said. "We have resources here. Why don't you consider yourself a consultant? Give me a direction, some idea where she might be hiding, and help guide the team I send out to find her."

If Drew's gut instinct was right and Addison was heading to her home turf, Thomas's team wouldn't stand a chance. The woman he'd known, the woman he'd planned to marry, had always been ferociously independent and smart as a whip. If she was on the run and didn't want to be found, there was only one place she'd go. And if anyone cornered her there, she'd strike first and ask for identification later.

"No." Resigned, Drew accepted his fate. He couldn't leave this to anyone else. Whether or not he was thrilled by the idea of seeing her again, he figured he was the only one with a chance of convincing her to come out of hiding. "I'll find her."

"That's the best news I've had since they dumped this on my desk," Thomas admitted.

"I'll need gear."

"We have the best."

"I'll need cash for a car and cell phone in addition to the travel expenses."

Thomas pursed his lips. "Done."

"I'll find Addison, but I can't promise to bring her in." He cut off Thomas's automatic protest. "We both know she won't be safe until Everett and that leak are contained. She knows that, too. I'll monitor the news and do my best, but don't count on a quick resolution where she's concerned."

"Agreed." Thomas pressed a button on his phone. "My assistant will show you downstairs. Take whatever you need to get the job done."

"Yes, sir." If he thought about timelines and proximity, he'd lose it. Reminding himself life was a day-to-day effort, he focused on the first step: gearing up.

The T-shirt, warm-up pants and sneakers weren't going to hold up to what amounted to a manhunt through some difficult terrain.

Drew turned in his seat when the door opened and stood up as the receptionist returned. If he was right, if he still knew the woman at all, he'd soon be face-to-face with Addison. Surreal was a vast understatement. He couldn't decide if he should be terrified or ecstatic at the prospect. He supposed her reaction would help him decide.

Chapter Three

Thomas pushed his chair away from his desk and stood, restless and uncertain about what he'd just set in motion.

Not so long ago he'd been given a second chance and reunited with the only woman he'd ever loved. His personal success should give him hope for Drew and Addison, but he couldn't quite drum up that elusive emotion for this situation. Sending Drew to track down Addison could backfire. Not just for the two of them—three if he counted the little boy—but for the integrity of the operational mess he'd inherited.

It seemed more and more challenging lately to think of his Specialists as assets. They were all capable and strong people who, at the end of the day, were here as tools to be applied to specific purposes and operations. It was a particular trial when the people he assigned, like Drew, weren't even part of his elite program.

Time to hand over the reins. He stared through

his big office window, blind to the stunning view. A knock sounded at his door. "Come in," he called without turning.

"I saw Bryant leave," Deputy Director Emmett Holt said. "Did he agree to help?"

Thomas loosened his tie as he returned to his desk chair. There was no need to stand on formality with Holt, who understood all too well what was riding on this operation.

"He agreed."

"But?" Holt sank into one of the visitors' chairs opposite Thomas. "You look like you've eaten bad fish."

"I feel a bit like that, to tell the truth. This could backfire. In a big way."

"Were there other options?"

Thomas drummed his fingers on the supple leather arm of his chair. "No." The whole reason they'd brought Drew into this was because Addison had disappeared. Completely. "But it's a lot to ask."

"He'll manage."

Thomas met Holt's sharp gaze. "I meant her. Addison's running for her life, for her son's life, and we're sending out a ghost to find her. She has no idea what happened—only that he never made it to their wedding."

"Then I stand corrected."

Thomas arched an eyebrow. "He won't manage?"

"No. *She* will manage."

It sounded like a magic-wand theory to Thomas's ears, and that was one theory everyone in his line of work always rejected. "He's not a trained Specialist."

"Oh, so that's the problem."

Thomas didn't like the half smile on Holt's face. "Explain."

"You feel guilty for sending an unqualified civilian after a high-value asset."

"That's not true." Where the hell was this coming from? He and Holt had different management styles, but this series of irritating questions wasn't typical. "Bryant might be a civilian now, but he could step in and train our recruits on anything at a moment's notice."

"So he's qualified."

"More than."

"Then I guess you're feeling guilty because we didn't have an equally qualified Specialist available?"

They both knew the roster and they both took great pride in the skills of the men and women on their team. "Why the hell are you being so difficult?"

"Because you need to ease up on yourself," Holt said, his expression somber. "The woman and her kid are missing, Everett escaped with some damned sophisticated help and you just sent out the best option for everyone involved."

"Thanks for the vote of confidence." Thomas wasn't sure how else to interpret that tidy speech.

"If that's what you need, you're welcome." Holt leaned forward. "We talked about it, looked at every asset before you brought Bryant in. He is the only choice for this mission."

Thomas knew that was correct. Even logical.

"Personally," Holt continued, "I believe he'll succeed, no matter how she reacts to seeing him again. He's resourceful. He'll bring her in or make sure we can."

"You're right," Thomas allowed, though he knew this decision would haunt him well into his retirement if it went wrong. He rubbed the palm of one hand with the opposite thumb. "I've never once forgotten that our Specialists are people. We demand more than we should—"

"But never more than we're willing to give ourselves," Holt finished for him. "That philosophy—*your* philosophy—is at the heart of our entire program. Don't ever doubt it."

"All right." Thomas raised his hands, palms out. There had been a time, not too long ago, when Thomas had doubted his philosophy and much more. He'd doubted Holt's loyalty to the Specialists and the nation at large. Been certain he'd made the wrong call naming Holt as the next director.

No longer. Holt had proved himself in the field and protected the Mission Recovery office during a complicated attack from one of Thomas's old enemies. Not only that, he'd recently become family by marrying Thomas's sister. "Thanks for the pep talk," he said, the burden feeling a bit lighter. "It's the kid," he added, finally articulating the real issue. He and Jo wanted to start a family soon, and although his wife was as independent and resourceful as Addison, Thomas knew how far he'd go if someone took aim at his wife or their children.

"I figured," Holt said with a sympathetic nod.

"Cecelia is expecting you and Jo to join the family for July Fourth weekend."

"We're looking forward to it," Thomas said, more relieved than he should be about the change of topic. "Jo is making noise about getting a boat of our own when I retire."

"Want me to keep an eye out for you?"

"A casual eye." He recognized Holt's method of shifting the topic to something more normal. "But I don't want her to know I'm looking yet."

"Lucky for you, I can keep a secret," Holt said, heading for the doorway.

"I'm well aware." Thomas smiled as Holt walked out, the guilt of Addison and Drew's situation muted. For now.

He'd needed the reminder that Holt provided. If

Drew had given the first sign that he'd cave under the pressure of the request, Thomas would've found another way to track down Addison.

As it was, he was back to hoping the reunion, although certain to be awkward and emotional, would result in capturing the traitorous Everett and the root of his network so Addison and her son could return to life without fear of retribution.

Chapter Four

In the fading light of another warm summer day, Addison came outside with two bowls of ice cream. Sitting next to Andy on the top step of the porch, she handed him one.

"We had ice cream last night."

"It's summer," Addison said with a smile. "And you've played hard all day. Besides, it won't keep forever." Her friend Nico, father of Bernadette, her best childhood friend, had given her permission to stay here in his mother's old place. He'd brought them out by boat and had delivered more supplies yesterday. Although she appreciated what the weather-worn shack provided, she didn't trust the ancient freezer on the back porch.

Andy didn't waste time arguing over the bonus treat and he dug in with enthusiasm.

As dark crept in from the edges of the swamp,

the insects ramped up with an evening chorus that rose and fell with the soft breeze. In the tall marsh grass across the water, fireflies took flight. "Look." She pointed toward the soft twinkling.

"Can I catch some? Nico told me kids here use them as night-lights."

"Not tonight." She was tired and wary despite being as alone as a person could be out here. Other than Nico's, she hadn't even heard another boat in the area for days, yet she felt edgy as if they were being watched. They'd been here for two weeks, and according to the news, Craig continued to evade authorities as the story of his illegal dealings came out in dribs and drabs. "I did that a few times when I was your age," she said to her son. "Even once during a campout right here."

"Really?" His eyes were wide.

"Mmm-hmm. Mama Leonie, Nico's mom, lived out here more than in town. Nico's daughter was my best friend and we used to come here every chance we got. There was only one room then."

"No bedroom?"

Addison shook her head. "She didn't want one."

"Where did she sleep?"

"Outside on the back porch." Addison looked around once more, picturing it as it had been. "I always thought it was the best tree house."

"But it's not *in* the tree. I think we should call it a swamp fort." Andy twisted around and then leaned forward to peer through the slatted porch to the water below. "I like this part hanging over the water."

"It keeps the rooms cooler."

"Huh."

Addison smiled to herself. The conversation relaxed her. Feeling watched was simply paranoia, which wasn't unexpected. Nico had assured her no one came out this way much since Leonie's death a few years back. He promised that she and Andy would be safe in the old Voodoo Queen's place. Few people knew this place was still habitable. More important, only two people knew that Addison knew about it.

"This is a real adventure, Mom." Andy scooped up another big bite of ice cream. "I saw a frog out there." He pointed with his spoon toward the edge of the water. "And an alligator down that way." The spoon moved down the shore, away from the house.

"Are you sure?"

He nodded, his mouth full and a sticky stain of chocolate bracketing its corners. "Nico showed me how to spot 'em."

"Did he?"

"Uh-huh."

"He's the expert." Nico knew these swamps

inside and out and stayed busy as a tour guide. When she'd knocked on his door in the middle of the night two weeks ago, he hadn't batted an eye at her request for help. Stomping into his boots, he'd taken her keys and driven her out to the edge of the swamp without asking any uncomfortable questions. After promising he wouldn't mention her arrival to anyone, he'd loaded two boats, tied them together and guided her out here. Once they'd unloaded and he was satisfied she had key supplies, he'd left her one boat and returned to his dock with the other.

She supposed other people might've felt obligated to help because she'd sent money back to help with Mama Leonie's health care and final expenses. But Nico lived by a different philosophy. You took care of your own, no matter how much time or silence passed between visits. That had shown through when he'd returned with a boatload of supplies at midday, and he'd clearly spent some important time with Andy while she'd put things away in the house.

Now they had a stock of wood and charcoal, a generator and fuel to keep the small luxuries like the freezer, the ancient water heater and the two lightbulbs inside the shack going. They couldn't stay here indefinitely, but they could certainly stay through the summer and longer if she hadn't figured out the next step by then.

"Mom, the swamp is kinda creepy at night."

She felt herself smiling. "In a good way?"

"Yeah!

"Nico told me his mom knew everything about the swamp."

"She sure did. And she loved to teach anyone who'd listen. She treated me like a granddaughter. I learned her secret recipe for pancakes when I turned ten."

Andy looked up at her. "Would she have been my grandma, too?"

"You better believe it. The two of you would've been best friends." She rubbed her hand across his small shoulders. "Leonie was very special. I loved coming out here to see her."

"This was your adventure place?"

Addison nodded. "Yes. And it's good to be back." More than she'd expected, really. It felt like home, even though she wasn't anywhere near the farm where she'd grown up in Mississippi.

"I think it's better than SeaWorld!"

"Just don't try and pet a gator." They shared a quiet laugh. "Tomorrow we can start exploring. I can show you what's—"

"Safe," Andy interrupted with a put-upon sigh. "You said we wouldn't have to be together the whole time on this adventure."

"I said we wouldn't have to be in the car the

whole time. And you've been playing on your own, right?"

"Right."

"I just want to be sure you know what to do or where to go if you come across something dangerous." Or someone.

Craig wouldn't have the first idea of how to find this place, shouldn't even know about it, but she wanted to be sure Andy knew how to find Nico in case they were somehow injured or separated.

"That doesn't sound like an adventure."

"Oh, it will be."

Water splashed nearby. Andy turned to her with wide eyes. "Was that a gator?"

"Probably not. Gators slide into the water and most of the time they hardly make a sound or even a ripple." A small exaggeration, but worth the resulting expression of wonder on his face. "A sound like that's usually a fish or frog." Not a person, she reminded herself. People who slipped or splashed made even more noise.

"Nico taught you that, didn't he?"

"Mmm-hmm." She held out her empty bowl, let him stack his on top. "Take those inside to the sink, please."

"Do I have to wash 'em?"

"No, sweetie. I'll do it after bedtime."

She listened to his small footsteps, waited

for the inevitable noise as the bowls and spoons landed with a clatter in the old porcelain sink. He rushed back out to join her a moment later, the screen door slapping shut behind him.

"About bedtime…"

She smiled into his serious face. "Yes?"

"It's summer, so there isn't such thing as a school night."

"I noticed."

"And we're on an adventure."

"We are." She knew where he was headed, but she waited for him to say what was on his mind.

"Could I not have a bedtime?"

She waited. This was the way they did things. He had to ask nicely even when he delivered sound reasons.

"Please," he added quickly with a winning smile.

"You still have a lot of growing to do," she pointed out. "Sleep is important for growing." Just after Christmas she'd bought him new tennis shoes, only to have him grow out of them within a few days. "Enough sleep," she amended, anticipating his next argument.

His face fell but only for a moment. "There were nights last summer that didn't have bedtime and we were at home."

"True." She drilled her finger at his belly, making him squeal and jump back. "There will be nights like that on our adventure, too."

"It's not even all the way dark yet."

"That doesn't mean it isn't late." And her son rose early, ready and eager for every day. She was more than a little grateful when she realized how well Nico had updated the place through the years. She wouldn't have to settle for instant coffee.

She patted the top step. "Come sit with me and we'll count the first stars."

Andy dropped down beside her, just a little sulky with his elbows on his knees and his chin propped on his fists.

"You can't see the stars if you're looking at the water."

He dutifully looked up, his lower lip poking out like a shelf. "Wow. There's lots up there already." Interested now, he forgot to pout.

They counted more than twenty as the sky transformed into an inky purple above the tall cypress trees. When she heard him yawn, she nudged him back inside the "swamp fort." Leaning against the doorway, she kept her weary little man on task as he chattered through the bedtime rituals.

The little things like pajamas and brushing teeth felt so normal even in Mama Leonie's rambling little shack. "Which one will it be tonight?"

She hefted the backpack full of comics onto the narrow bed near his feet.

His eyebrows drew together as he considered. "Will you tell me more about Mama Leonie?"

Surprised, she agreed. "Where do you want me to start?"

"Why did she live out here all alone?"

Addison gathered her thoughts, drew hard on her memory to recall the tales. She didn't want to scare Andy with voodoo stories, but she didn't want to paint Leonie as anything other than the wonderful woman she'd been.

"Nico's mama didn't live out here alone all the time. She raised Nico and his brothers and sisters closer to town."

Andy stared at the little room. "Because the swamp fort was too small?"

"Partly."

"Why not just make it bigger?"

"They already had a bigger house. Maybe I'll take you by it one day." Addison settled on the edge of the bed while Andy squished himself and his pillow into a comfortable position. Going through the familiar motions soothed her. "But she always had this place for herself."

"So it was her adventure place."

"In a manner of speaking, I suppose you're right. Mama Leonie came out here to meet with people who needed things. She practiced a religion called voodoo."

"She turned people into zombies?" Andy's eyes went wide as saucers but with more excitement than fear. Addison hoped it would always be that way, the opportunity for discovery outweighing potential distress.

"Of course not. She was smart and kind and full of compassion for people. She was more like a doctor or therapist."

"But voodoo has zombies."

"Comic books have voodoo zombies." Addison wondered if she needed to rein him in a bit. "In real life, voodoo isn't nearly so creepy." She walked her fingers over his foot and up his leg and tickled him behind the knee. He giggled and squirmed out of reach. "It's complicated but interesting, and the people around her counted on Leonie like they would a doctor or therapist." She stood and managed to kiss his forehead before he could protest. "Now get some sleep."

"Like a zombie?"

"If it helps you grow," she said with a laugh.

"Where are you sleeping?"

"I'll put my sleeping bag in here with you. After I take care of the dishes."

"And your quiet time."

That habit was one definite success in her parenting career. As soon as Andy had been old enough to understand, she'd taught him to appreciate the quiet time she needed in the evenings. "That's right. Now quit stalling and go to sleep."

"Did Mama Leonie ever do voodoo on you?" Andy asked before she could get out the door.

"Maybe I'll tell you that story tomorrow night."

"Ah, come on."

"Stalling. Love you, bear."

"Love you, too," he muttered, clearly resigned to losing the battle for more of a story.

She left the door cracked, the same way she did at home. It was a small compromise for him, but an added measure of security for her under these new circumstances.

At home during quiet time she would've heated water for tea and pulled out some reading for work or pleasure. Here, hot tea meant lighting the wood-burning stove or the grill outside. On such a sultry evening, it didn't feel like a good idea to fill the kitchen with more heat. And she hesitated to start a fire in the grill at this hour.

Among the supplies Nico had delivered was a jug of homemade wine. She poured some into one of the mason jars that served as drink ware and carefully sipped. The sweet, light taste was a pleasant surprise and she bravely sipped a second time.

She washed and dried the dishes, stacking them back with the others on the open corner shelves near the small table. As a youngster she'd often been entrusted with this chore and had used a chair instead of a stepstool to get the job done.

The memories flooded through her, warm and comfortable, and for a fleeting moment she could almost hear the lilting voices filling the room with chatter and laughter. There had been good times here, each of them precious to her.

The creative "architecture" in the bayous was the polar opposite of the sleek designer spaces she'd left behind, and Addison found her fondness for this little shack and rugged natural surroundings hadn't changed. She'd learned early, from her own humble beginnings, that the value wasn't in the furnishings of a place, but the people who filled it.

Mama Leonie and her family by blood and choice had filled this place with love, encouragement and hope. *Still filled it,* Addison thought as a breeze ruffled the curtains at the window over the sink. For the first time since leaving the West Coast, she felt a sliver of doubt about running here. She didn't want to ruin the healthy vibe or cause any trouble for Nico and his family. The locals still revered this place because of all the good Leonie had done for them, but Craig wouldn't care about any of that. If he found her, he'd have no respect for the history and simply level whatever stood between him and her.

Too bad he'd never understand the biggest gap was full of intangibles, not physical obstacles.

"Mama Leonie, if you can hear me," Addison whispered, "I don't want to bring you trouble. There was nowhere else to go." Truly. Nowhere else Craig didn't know about. She looked down, twisting the engagement ring on her finger. What a fool she'd been to share so much of her life, of herself, with a man capable of such crimes. Why hadn't she seen through him? "I'm sorry if trouble follows me," she murmured into the silence. "Any help you can send would be appreciated."

She took off the ring and stuffed it in her pocket, scowling at the pale indentation left behind on her finger. The mark would fade and, with the bright days of summer, the pale line would soon fill in with healthy color. She'd taken a stand, done the right thing, and she had to trust the authorities to deal with Craig the right way. Soon.

Though her specialty was corporate law, she understood Craig and his legal defense team would make the most of every loophole available. Knowing the system too well to trust it blindly, she'd taken that final precaution and had mailed extra information on to a neutral party.

Addison paused at the cracked door, hearing Andy's steady breathing. They were out of harm's way. *Safe.* She repeated the word as she carried her glass of wine to the hammock on the back porch, screened in thanks to Nico's hard work.

Letting the hammock swing her gently, she reviewed every detail of her discovery, her report and her escape, looking for missteps, for anything Craig might twist to his advantage.

He could drag her into it by association, but she'd never had anything to do with his dealings. Although her firm hadn't balked at her request for six weeks off, she knew it was only a matter of time before she was unemployed. Her firm wouldn't tolerate the bad publicity of having her name dragged through the mud because she'd been idiot enough to nearly marry a traitor. Smart women weren't supposed to fall for the wolf in sheep's clothing. Her only saving grace was she'd found out before exchanging vows, but that wouldn't be enough to save her job.

She tipped back more of the wine, draining the glass, considering another glass. To pour or not to pour? became the most pertinent question. She used a toe to push off and send the hammock rocking again while she made up her mind.

It was so peaceful out here, the darkness so deep and quiet. She'd loved the West Coast city life, loved the challenges and perks of a high-powered, well-paying job. Being a single parent of an active, intelligent son had ups and downs, but at the end of every day, there was unconditional love. Everything about that life, except her son, was over. Where did that leave her? Where did she *want* to go next?

Money wasn't a big, immediate problem. Having been raised on next to nothing, she'd invested well and saved more through the years. Only Bernadette, as the executor of Addison's will and potential guardian for Andy, had access to those accounts.

She rubbed at the space between her eyebrows, wishing once more that there had been a way to warn Bernadette of the oncoming storm. But that kind of move would've been dangerous. During her relationship with Craig, she'd mentioned a few of their young and stupid antics in New Orleans, and he'd taken care of Andy six months ago when she and Bernadette had spent a girls' weekend in Tahoe.

Did fools come any bigger than she'd been with Craig?

Rolling to her feet, Addison headed back inside with her mason jar. She'd done all she could, taken every precaution, including running here, the safest place she knew. There was nothing left to do but wait it out. She had nearly six weeks left before school started. Out here, with only Nico as a contact, surely that would be enough time for her to know how much farther she'd have to run to provide Andy with as normal a life as possible.

Walking inside, she closed the door and checked the load on the shotgun. It had felt odd in her hands at first, but after a few hours of practice, shooting at stationary targets and then moving ones, her hands and body remembered the routine.

Carrying the shotgun with her, she unrolled her sleeping bag on the kitchen side of the narrow bedroom doorway. Settling on top of the thick layers of fabric for the remainder of the night, Addison listened to the soft hum of the refrigerator. It seemed to underscore the gentle, content sounds of her son sleeping on the cot in the corner on the other side of the door.

Bugs continued whirring and chirping outside, and she heard the occasional splash from fish, frog or turtle beneath the stilted house. They were safe. Craig couldn't find them here. If he searched anywhere, he was more likely to start with the small plot of land in Mississippi that still held her name on the title. It was on public record, which she couldn't change now. Although he knew she'd loved visiting New Orleans, she'd never told him anything about her dirt-stained summers out here in the bayou.

Nico had promised to keep her presence here a secret as well as keep her informed of any suspicious strangers who might appear and ask questions. She had the radio, and maybe in a week or two she'd risk a trip into town to scour the internet for any warning signs and check in with Professor Hastings.

Addison discarded the idea immediately. Any contact with her friend and mentor earlier than planned would put her "insurance policy" in jeopardy. No one could know she'd sent him backup files of Craig's treacherous dealings as well as more incriminating evidence. She thought of all the names she didn't know on his contact lists, the lists she'd downloaded from his phone and computer before sending them anonymously to the FBI.

With any luck, they would keep that as an ace up their sleeve, the secret weapon he wouldn't be prepared to explain away in court. Combined with what she'd sent to Professor Hastings, Craig would never be free long enough to cause trouble for her or Andy. As long as they caught him.

As she drifted off to sleep, one hand on the stock of the shotgun, she almost believed it.

Minutes or hours later, Addison woke with a start. It was tricky, listening past the blood thudding in her ears, to figure out what had startled her. The refrigerator was quiet and she heard the creak of wind in the trees.

Not the wind, she realized, as the curtains over the sink were still. She strained for another clue, telling herself it was just another overreaction to new surroundings.

This time the quiet splash of water under the house was followed immediately by the soft rasp of a boat being pulled onto the grasses that lined the shore. Damn it all to hell. Someone had found her.

Immediate worry for Nico flashed through her. Guilt pricked her conscience. Had they hurt him to get a lead on her direction? Since Leonie's death, there had been no reason to head into this part of the swamp. Many of the locals believed she haunted the place, and they preferred to avoid even benevolent ghosts.

Addison gripped the shotgun and sat up without making a sound. It might very well be someone familiar with the shack and in need of shelter. If they'd noticed the generator was going, it made sense to stop and ask for help, but Addison prepared to shoot first and ask questions later.

For several long moments nothing more than typical night swamp sounds reached her. Maybe whoever had been in the boat just needed to sleep off a wrong turn. It happened, and hospitality was part of the odd society out here. If they stayed down there with the boat, they wouldn't have any trouble from her.

She'd just relaxed her hold on the gun when she caught the unmistakable creaking tread of the third step in the string leading to the porch. Addison tried to breathe, telling herself Craig wouldn't come by night and sure as hell wouldn't come to a place so rural without vocalizing his discomfort in the process.

But that had been the Craig she'd known—thought she'd known—not the greedy bastard who'd brokered terrible deals that ended with dead US citizens.

She listened, her palms going damp as whoever was outside climbed closer to the porch. Part of her wanted to run, to grab Andy and bolt through the back, but she'd only heard one person. She could take one person.

"Addison?"

The inquiry, delivered in a low whisper, only revealed that the speaker was male. Nico would've announced himself already, knowing she was armed and prepared to defend herself.

So who else out here could possibly know her name?

The intruder made no secret of his approach now. He leaned close to the window. "Addison? Are you in there?"

Without a porch light, the intruder's identity was impossible to make out, but he was nearly at the door.

"Hello?" The voice, a little stronger, sounded familiar. "Addi?"

Addison's heart clutched. She knew that voice, and only one man had ever called her by that nickname. Drew Bryant, her long-dead fiancé.

She shook her head. Clearly she'd let the stress and worry get to her. Drew wasn't here, wasn't even alive. This was probably just a vivid dream induced by Andy's talk of zombies. She took a deep breath and let it out slowly, urging her brain to wake up.

The screen-door hinges squealed and the handle of the main door turned. *A dream,* she thought, *it has to be a dream.* No one but Nico knew she was here. As the door eased open, Addison leveled the shotgun at the man casting shadows across the weak moonlight spilling through the door.

"Addi, it's me, Drew. I'm here to help."

Wake up!

Addison fired. The loud report deafened her to the splintering wood as the buckshot pelted the front door. The reactions of the stranger in front of her were like a bad mime, first ducking behind the door, then rushing forward and taking the gun before she could fire again.

"It's *me*," he said, his voice lost in the ringing in her ears.

The single lightbulb came on and she covered her mouth, barely smothering the scream lodged in her chest. "No. *No.*" This wasn't possible. It was a cruel twist of her overwrought imagination. She pushed to her feet, away from the man with Drew's face. Any second now she'd wake up from this horrible nightmare.

"Mommy?" It was her son's tiny voice that ripped through her confusion and brought her back to her senses. She had to protect Andy at all costs.

"I'm here, Andy." She couldn't decide. Comfort her son or confront the man in front of her.

"Take care of him." The man carefully leaned the gun against the wall closest to her. "Then I'll explain and you can shoot me if you want to."

It was such a Drew thing to say that she followed her instincts and tended to Andy.

"Why did the gun go off? Are we in trouble?"

"Someone startled me, that's all." She ushered her boy back into bed and pulled the covers up tight. "It's late. Go back to sleep."

"Who is that?" He rubbed his eyes.

"An unexpected friend." It was a simpler answer than explaining her possible hallucinations. "He doesn't want to hurt us." Apparitions and hallucinations didn't have enough substance to hurt anyone. She hoped. Whoever—whatever—was out there, he'd taken the gun from her all too easily. "He startled me and I fired the gun, that's all."

"I'm scared."

"That's understandable," she said with more

calm than she felt with her heart pounding. "But I won't let anything bad happen. In the morning I'll tell you the whole story." Assuming she'd know the story by then. At least it gave her a bit of time to think of something logical.

They both gave the doorway a look when they heard the scrape of a chair across the wood floor.

"Promise?"

She pressed a kiss to his brow and wrapped him in a big hug. "I promise." Holding her son in her arms and smelling the sweet scent of his hair, she knew this wasn't a bizarre, unbelievable nightmare. The man in the kitchen might really be Drew. She tensed. If so, he owed her a detailed explanation.

"You'll tell me if I need to find Nico, right?" he whispered into her ear.

Her heart slammed against her ribs. She couldn't imagine sending her little boy into the swamp, even if they had talked about that very scenario as a safety precaution. "That's not necessary this time, especially not in the dark," she said. "For now I need you to stay right here in this bed." She leaned back, held his shoulders as she looked him in the eye. "Promise me."

Andy promised, gave her another fierce hug and released her to deal with the man in the kitchen.

Chapter Five

Drew heard the low voices in the other room and felt like an ass for his clumsy entrance. His hands shook and not from dodging the shotgun blast. He trembled for her. If there'd ever been any doubt, he knew for sure that he'd lost everything in that POW camp. Years of his life, sure, but so much more.

Addison seemed to grow more beautiful every time he saw her. Remembering her radiance the day before their wedding had carried him through those dark days in unthinkable conditions. Seeing her playing with her new family in the park had filled him with jealousy and later—much later—with a weird sense of peace. She'd found her place, the happy life she'd dreamed of, even if it was without him. And just now, despite the messy hair, her face pale with shock, the shorts and oversize T-shirt concealing the sweet curves of her body, he looked at her and saw the prettiest woman on the planet.

Not that he could tell her, even if he hadn't mishandled this completely. She wasn't his. He'd let her go, let her keep believing he was dead. He should've stayed in the boat under the house and waited until morning to talk to her. But he'd needed to see her.

He told himself the confirmation was required for the job. Waiting until morning and protecting people who might not need it was a waste of time and resources. He pulled a chair away from the kitchen table, sat down and tried to believe the lie.

No sale. Director Casey might've pulled him out of Detroit, but the official case had nothing to do with why he'd come out here in the dark. He hadn't come here for Casey. He'd climbed those steps and disrupted Addison's night simply to satisfy his curiosity.

Behind him the door opened and he felt her staring at him.

She crossed the room, keeping as much distance as the small space allowed. "This is impossible. You're real." She cleared her throat. "Alive, I mean."

"I am."

"Part of me expected you to vaporize while I talked with..." She tilted her head back toward the door. "With my son."

So the boy he'd seen in the park was hers, not Everett's. He wasn't sure why that made him feel worse about all this. "Leaving you on our wedding day wasn't my idea."

"And still you weren't there." She held up her hands as if she could wave away the accusation. "Forget it. We can't change whatever took you away. I was grateful you left the note."

He'd broken protocol with that, but he'd had to do something. It was their wedding day, for crying out loud. The note wouldn't have been nearly enough to earn her understanding, but it had been the only option.

"Come on, Drew. Start explaining."

Start where? Words failed him. His life had been a thousand times easier staying away from her. Lonely as hell, but easier. She'd moved on, had a kid, and the best way to honor her independence was to move on with his. He focused on his purpose here: to get her into Casey's protection.

"Speaking of vaporizing," he began, pointing at her. He realized the error of the phrase when her eyes narrowed dangerously. "Some important people are worried about you and your son." Casey couldn't have warned him about that detail? Where was the kid's father? "They asked me if I could track you down."

"What kind of important people?"

"People who want to keep you safe."

She pursed those full, rosy lips, then shook her head. "Congratulations. You of all people should know I came here because I didn't want to be found. Tell them you were wrong. Tell them you couldn't find me."

"Not a chance. I can't go back empty-handed."

"Of course you can. You *will*, since I'm not going anywhere with you."

"Be reasonable, Addison."

"You first," she snapped, carefully pitching her voice so she wouldn't wake her son. "Tell me who sent you."

"You need help. You're in over your head."

"Give me a name, Drew."

He hesitated. "You've got the authorities running in circles looking for you all over the country," he hedged. Based on her mutinous expression, she wouldn't budge on this. The only name he could give wouldn't mean anything to her anyway. He weighed the mission goal with the usual security requirements. "Thomas Casey sent me."

"Alone?"

Drew nodded, wondering why she was so insistent about this.

"Who is he to you?"

"No one." He jerked a shoulder. "A man who gets what he wants. He sent an escort to pick me up in Detroit—"

"Detroit, *Michigan*?"

Inside his head, Drew swore. Was there anything he could do right here? "Yes."

"You've been living in the States?"

"Yes."

"You're not dead. You're living back in your hometown."

"Yes," he whispered, feeling miserable for causing the pain in her soft icy-blue eyes.

"For how long?"

He might as well lay out all the cards. "I've been in Detroit almost a year."

She turned her back on him. "Get out."

"I can't do that." How could he make her understand? Without her trust, he wasn't sure he could get her to cooperate, and he didn't want to resort to brute force.

She whirled around, her blue gaze full of fury and fire. "Sure you can. You've been in Detroit, letting me believe you were dead. You seem to have mastered staying out of my life. Feel free to continue."

His temper bubbled up to match hers. "It wasn't my idea to change the status quo." Irrational or not, she had a son. Not a baby or even a toddler— the kid was in grade school. "You didn't wait too damn long to get on with your life after the wedding," he said, pointing toward the closed door.

She reeled back as if he'd hit her and her voice turned brittle. "You can't stay here."

"I have to." He struggled for any remnant of sanity. His world, barely held together since his release, was breaking apart now that he was in the same room with her. "You need me."

"No, I don't," she countered. "I'm doing just fine on my own."

"Really? Craig Everett escaped federal custody."

"Shh." Panic flashed across her face as she glanced at the door. "He doesn't know anything yet."

"So Everett is the kid's father?"

Her gaze turned hard as she glared at him again. "I know he escaped and I guarantee if he'd walked in that door—" she stabbed a finger in that direction "—if it had been anyone else but you, my aim would've been right on target."

He believed her. He'd seen her in action on a shooting range. Years ago. "So you missed because it was me?"

"Yes."

He accepted the admission as a small positive sign. "We can go our separate ways after I get you safely out of Ev—his reach."

"How? Witness protection?"

"Possibly." He didn't know the details, but he trusted Casey with the task.

"No deal."

"Addi, be reasonable."

"I am being reasonable. As well as responsible. You don't have any idea just how connected Craig is. Witness protection won't be enough and it isn't fair to my son."

"Thomas Casey can keep you both safe."

"He's in some branch of government?"

"He is."

"No deal."

Drew bit back another string of foul words. "You're infuriating."

"Same goes for you." She crossed the room to the refrigerator, opened the door and bent to look inside. He tried to ignore the view as the soft fabric of her shorts hugged her backside.

"I think this is our first real fight," he said.

"Hardly," she muttered, handing him a bottle of water. "But it can be our last. Take this for the road."

"I'm not leaving." He twisted off the plastic cap and leaned back in his chair. "We never fought before...our wedding day." He forced the last two words out and then took a long drink of water.

"We fought plenty in the days and months after. You just weren't there."

"I'm sorry, Addi. If I could change it..."

"It was our *wedding* day," she whispered. "Why did they need *you*?"

His heart seized at the pain in her voice. Raw and fresh, she sounded exactly the way he felt every day. When he'd agreed to help Director Casey, he'd known her reaction would be volatile at best. He hadn't been prepared to deal with how much his appearance would hurt her. As she'd moved on with her life, he hadn't expected her to feel anything but initial shock at seeing him again.

But she didn't look like a woman who'd moved on, despite the evidence he'd seen for himself. Top of her field, gorgeous home in the right neighborhood and a son. That was the piece that slid like a knife between his ribs, straight to his heart. During his time as a prisoner, he'd fantasized about making love with Addi, about the family they would build in years to come.

She'd done that. With some other man.

"Why, Drew?"

He'd often asked the same thing and never found a decent answer. "I had the misfortune of knowing the key players in the area. Command said they needed me."

Her eyes went wide. "That's not what I call an explanation."

"It's the best I can offer."

With a derisive snort, she paced the small room, pausing near the front door. She pushed her hands into her hair. "You're supposed to be dead."

He wanted to take her in his arms and show

her how alive he felt. How alive she made him feel now that he could hear her voice, smell the light citrus of her shampoo. He wrapped one palm around the other fist, massaging the tension in his hands. "For a time that's what I wanted, too."

"I didn't say I wanted you to be dead." She pushed loose strands of her golden hair behind her ears. "I heard the news from your dad. His face…" She gazed up at the slanted tin-roof ceiling. "He's the one who told me you'd died."

"You saw my dad?" He swallowed the swell of grief that came with every thought of his father.

"Sure." She nodded. "We spoke frequently after the interrupted wedding. He apologized to me that it didn't go as scheduled." She leaned back against the big sink and propped one foot on the other.

The pose transported him back to the days when she'd stand just that way, waiting for the first cup of coffee to kick her into gear in the morning. He'd counted on a lifetime of moments like this one, but fate had dealt him a different hand.

"And I saw him again about two months after that," she added.

Two months. It still bothered him the way the army had handled his capture. "They didn't waste any time pronouncing me dead."

"They being the army, I assume?"

He nodded.

"Are you surprised?"

"Not really." What surprised him was how much he struggled not to touch her. He wanted a rewind button, a way to go back and say no to that cursed assignment, no matter the consequences. "That kind of risk, the emergency operation, went with the job."

Her eyebrows shot up. "Past tense?"

"Yes." He looked away from the softer sympathy in her eyes.

"But they still tapped you to come find me."

"Not in a military capacity. The army decided I wasn't fit for duty anymore."

"What the hell?" Her eyes raked him from head to toe. "Who made that decision?"

"Addi, the details aren't relevant right now."

"Of course they are," she insisted. "If you're not fit for service, why would this Casey person call you?"

"My kind of luck. The sooner I get you to him, the sooner we can get back to our lives." Separate lives, if that was what she wanted.

"You seem eager," she said. She came over and took the chair across from his at the table. "What kind of life do you have to get back to?"

Not the kind he wanted, that was for damn sure. In the weak light he caught another glimpse of the thin gold chain she wore, but whatever charms were on it were hidden by the T-shirt. Early in their relationship, he'd given her a heart charm inscribed with their initials and the date they'd met. He was a sap for hoping she still wore it.

"Drew?"

He didn't want to talk about himself. His life was vacant, nothing but loss and heartache. Hers mattered more. "What kind of life did you leave?"

Her lip curled. "I left an illusion," she said. "And I won't let myself fall into the same trap again."

What the hell did that mean? "You can't stay out here forever."

"I could," she argued. "But I don't need forever. And I sure don't need the certain failure of federal protection if they can't keep a traitor behind bars."

"All right. What's the plan?"

"That's none of your concern."

"I'm making it my concern."

She laughed, a bitter edge in the soft sound, as she propped her foot on the seat of the chair. He watched her run her fingertips over a small scar near her kneecap.

The blast of worry over an obvious sign of surgery was just one more irrational reaction added to the rest, but he couldn't stop himself from asking her what had happened.

"Nothing major. I tweaked it on a ski trip in Tahoe."

"When?"

"A couple years ago."

He should've been there. For everything. "I didn't know you liked to ski."

"Neither did I. It was a girls' weekend kind of thing."

Why did that flood him with so much relief? "I was in the middle of a rec league basketball game when Casey picked me up."

"Oh?"

"Since I, um, got back, I got involved a bit with the old neighborhood."

"Following in your dad's footsteps?"

Drew shrugged. "It was a starting point."

She bit her lip and pressed the back of her hand to the corner of her eye. "He was a good man, Drew." She cleared her throat. "The news of your death just tore him up."

"It tore me up when I heard about his heart attack," he confessed. "Long after the fact."

She shifted in her chair once more, her hand reaching across the small table, but she caught herself before making contact.

Smart, he thought. And he was grateful one of them had been. He couldn't be sure how he'd react to her touch. "You need to get some rest before we set out tomorrow," he said, standing.

"I'm not going anywhere with you."

"Staying here is certain suicide."

"How do you figure that? Unless you were followed, I'll be fine."

She had him there. Why couldn't he come up with a logical, convincing argument? Oh, yeah. He was distracted and overwhelmed by everything from her voice to her fierce determination. Watching her that day in the park had been bad, but this...this was a thousand times worse.

"I wasn't followed." His skills weren't that rusty. That strange sensation of being in two places at once, the phenomenon he'd first encountered in that damned prison cell, crept up on him now. It was something the shrinks discovered and referred to as a critical risk. Losing it here and now wasn't an option. He couldn't let his weakness put her and the kid in jeopardy.

With a deep, slow breath, he met her gaze once more. "I wasn't followed," he repeated when she continued to stare at him. "But I'd rather not deal with the swamp again tonight. I'll sleep down by the boat and we can discuss this in the morning."

ADDISON COULDN'T STOP staring at him, cataloging the differences between then and now. He'd always been fit, but now he looked as though he could afford to pack a few more pounds on that wide-shouldered frame. Plenty of definition in his arms and rippling under the snug dark T-shirt, but it wasn't quite *him*. She found the biggest changes in his face. Deep lines framed his eyes and mouth, and the tension in his jaw made her think he never quit clenching his teeth. What had he been through that had turned a strong, confident man into someone so haunted, hard and grim? She wasn't sure she wanted to know.

Dreamlike didn't begin to cover this. Her heart was stuck on "how" and "why" with frequent trips over questions about his new personal life. None of that mattered in the middle of the night in the bayou. She couldn't afford to let it matter come morning, either, but she could only win one battle at a time. It took all her willpower to push the right words past her lips. "You can't stay here."

"I can't leave."

She crossed her arms, fingernails digging into her biceps so she wouldn't reach for him again. Too tempting and far too risky. She suspected any physical contact would have her craving more, exactly as it had been between them from the moment they'd met. "You have to." If he stayed, she would lean on him. Worse, she would collapse or cling. Neither option was acceptable.

"Addi, sweetheart. You don't have to do this alone."

Again her heart tripped over the nickname, the sensation compounded by the familiar endearment and the sincerity shining in his brown eyes. "You have to go, Drew."

"Not in the dark."

"You made it here in the dark," she said ungraciously.

"Bad timing," he admitted. "And I did it for you. The same reason applies now. I'm not leaving until we reach an understanding."

She closed her eyes and counted to ten, remembering his mile-wide stubborn streak. Not unlike his son, when the man dug in, he wouldn't be budged.

Another worrisome thought chased the others through her mind. He didn't seem to know much about her and her son. Their son. Was it an act to throw her off? The obligations—personal and legal—niggled at her. Drew had a right to know Andy was his. "Fine. Take the hammock outside. We'll figure this out in the morning."

"The hammock," he repeated.

She cocked an eyebrow and stared him down in the same way she managed Andy when he was in a belligerent mood. "Screened porch. You found me. I trust you can find it."

"You won't try and sneak away?"

"Not unless you've suddenly become a sound sleeper." When they'd been together, it seemed he'd always slept with one eye open and his body ready to leap into action. She suppressed a needy shiver. Any kind of action.

"I wish," he muttered.

"So go on. We'll be here when you wake up."

With obvious reluctance, he walked out of the tiny cabin. She waited, listening to his soft footfalls as he walked across the rough planking to the other side of the cabin. When she heard the squeak of the hammock ropes, she turned out the lights.

Then she picked up the shotgun and moved her sleeping bag to Andy's side of the bedroom door. It was an immense relief to hear her son's soft, even breaths, confirming he hadn't been listening at the door the whole time.

Drew was alive. Her heart soared while her mind raced. What the hell was she supposed to do now? Drew was set on helping her, but she didn't see how his presence changed anything.

It infuriated her that her first instinct was to trust him. It was practically second nature to trust him, yet he'd been stateside all this time and had never reached out to her. That was the piece that cut so deeply and made her wary.

She knew the kind of friends Craig had on his side, knew he'd be scouring the country for any sign of her. If Craig's contacts—the ones who'd surely helped him escape—had any link to this Thomas Casey, she was screwed.

She heard a noise and held her breath, praying fervently it wasn't more trouble. Tonight had given her one surprise too many. Whatever she'd heard didn't repeat itself, but she listened closely just in case.

Drew was *alive*. Her heart rejoiced even as she resented him for staying away.

She couldn't tell illusion from reality, didn't trust her intuition when it came to men anymore. Had the love and affection she remembered so fondly with Drew been real? She pulled the necklace from under her shirt and ran the two charms along the fine gold chain. Why would a man who loved her the way he'd once claimed stay away?

On top of that, a woman didn't get more wrong about a man than she'd been about Craig. The floor creaked as she shifted, trying to get comfortable.

"Mama?"

"I'm here," she answered her son's sleepy voice. "You're safe."

"'Kay."

As she stared in the direction of the ceiling, she vowed—again—to keep him safe. Physically and emotionally.

From the near-miss nasty stepfather and the unexpected arrival of his real dad, Addison knew keeping that vow would be a serious challenge.

Chapter Six

A few hours later, Drew came fully awake in an instant when he heard voices and movement inside the small shack. Calm voices, no sounds of struggle or distress. Sitting up, he scrubbed at his face. The hammock wasn't to blame for his bleary eyes and lousy mood. He'd survived far worse in years past. No, his current frustration, physically and with the mission, had everything to do with the woman on the other side of a very thin wall.

He wanted to kick down that wall along with all the others she'd built against him over the years. How could he have been thinking only of her while she'd forgotten about him? The killed-in-action report had an impact on her choices, he knew, and it was irrational to hold that against her. But being right here with her... Was it so much to ask that she want him, too?

Hinges creaked on the screen door and he listened to her soft steps come around the corner.

Not wanting to advertise his past, he grabbed his T-shirt and covered the scars from his POW days.

She stayed on the other side of the torn screen wall, her arms folded across her chest. "You're still here."

"Told you I would be." He should never have agreed to this. Should've taken the offer to consult Casey's search. In a figure-hugging tank and cutoff denim shorts, her body was shown to perfection today. He'd always loved her generous curves, but it was clear she'd been putting in hours to keep herself strong and fit. He wanted to look away but couldn't stop staring. "Are you ready to get going?"

She shook her head. "Do you have to start in on that again?"

"Yes."

"No," she said, rubbing her finger where her engagement ring should've been. "Can't this wait? Coffee is brewing and breakfast will be ready shortly."

"Breakfast?" he echoed.

"Most important meal of the day, right? We can hash this out after we eat." She tilted her head. "I've got everything ready for Andy's favorite, pancakes and scrambled eggs."

The statement gave him a chill. Add a side of bacon and it would've been his favorite breakfast, too. How could she stand there as if it were a normal, everyday thing to have pancakes and eggs in the middle of the swamp when an escaped traitor was hunting her? "I need…" He coughed, clearing away the swell of emotions clogging his throat. "I need to check the perimeter."

There, that was much better than blurting out the needs his body urged him to share. What he'd noticed about her last night became more obvious in the clear morning light: her classic, Southern beauty hadn't faded a bit. It hadn't been artificially enhanced by his infatuation and unfulfilled longing or the poor lighting last night.

"You think someone followed you?" Her eyes went wide.

He cursed himself for worrying her. "No." The attraction, the damned pull of her, the need to protect, rode him as hard as ever. Annoyed, he stomped into his boots with more force than necessary, and the planked floorboards rattled. "But it's my job to keep you safe, and I'm going to do my job the right way. You've been here long enough for people to start talking."

"No one's talking about me. No one knows me out here anymore."

"Addi," he warned.

She held up her hands. "Fine."

He recognized the loaded delivery behind that single word. "If no one's onto you, it won't take me long to check."

"Are you okay?"

"Yeah." He scrubbed his hands over his face, remembering a few lazy mornings when they'd shared coffee and the paper in bed. Maybe they'd moved too fast back then and would already have burned each other out. He didn't believe it, but thanks to the damned assignment, he'd never know. "Hold a pancake for me."

"Andy's out of the bathroom if you want to grab a shower before the, um, perimeter thing."

"There's a bathroom?"

She laughed, the delighted sound washing over him, soothing him. "Nico made a few improvements despite his mother's simple wishes. The pump keeps a decent water pressure."

"Swamp guide and engineer."

"All Cajun," she said with a shrug.

"Yeah." He remembered the stories she'd shared with him. "I'll grab a shower when I'm back." He wasn't about to get stuck with his pants down—literally—until he knew they were safe. "Do you have a bug-out bag ready?"

"A what?"

"An emergency kit," he explained. "In case you have to run?"

She rubbed one bare foot up and down her shin. "We didn't bring that much along to begin with."

"I'll take care of it," he said. "If I'm not back in twenty minutes, I want the two of you to leave."

"And go where?"

"Deeper into the swamp. You'll figure out something."

"Drew—"

With his hand on the screen door between them, he hesitated, waiting for her to move. He needed even this small shield between them or he couldn't be responsible for the fallout. He wanted to hold her nearly as much as he wanted to keep breathing. "I'll be back in twenty."

"All right." She turned around, heading back into the cabin.

He couldn't take his eyes off the soft swing of her hips as she strolled away. He couldn't pull his mind back from the days when she'd welcomed his touch, when they'd held hands and talked about their hopes for the future.

"Hey," he called out.

She paused, glancing back over her shoulder.

"You didn't go the legal aid route. To the JAG office," he added at her blank look.

"They have no jurisdiction over Craig's dealings."

"No. Back then."

"Oh. A lot of things changed after…" She reached for her necklace.

The unspoken words were rattling through his mind. He knew she blamed him. He shouldered that old responsibility along with the new ones heaped on him by Director Casey. Trudging down the rickety steps while Addison ducked inside, he put his mind into guard-and-protect mode. No sense dwelling on what he couldn't have.

When he'd gone out to San Francisco and seen her with the man and boy, he'd known the fantasy that had carried him through his days as a prisoner was just that—fantasy. He didn't regret those fantasies; he'd just struggled to find his purpose without the army's guidance or Addison's support.

The youth center in his old neighborhood was up and running now, the renovation time shortened by his absolute lack of distraction. Absolute lack of a personal life. Drew checked the boat, pleased to find his gear still tied in place. Above him, he heard the muted voices of mother and son, and another flare of jealousy scorched his already raw heart.

"Focus," he muttered. He might be the only man on Earth able to find Addi, and that made him the only man who could keep her alive. He could radio his position to Casey's team or switch on one of the transmitters, but it would be one more thing on her list of unforgivables. Drew didn't want that. For either of them.

Coming in at dusk, watching and waiting until full dark to make his presence known, he hadn't been able to set much beyond the cursory alerts around the area. A calculated risk, but he'd been extremely cautious as he'd made a circuitous way through the bayou to Mama Leonie's famous shack.

Walking quietly along the water's edge, he kept an eye out for alligators or the more vicious human predators. He scanned the trees, keeping a careful mental record of where and when the shack was in view. He had a few dreamworthy gadgets from Casey's department, but he wasn't willing to blow them all at once. He wanted to give her protection without leaving a road map for Everett's connections. Anyone who could successfully stage an escape and avoid recapture for this long was undeniably dangerous.

Addison might think she was okay out here, she might believe Everett wouldn't bother beyond a cursory search of her hometown in Mississippi, but Casey felt differently. Making a home in the bayou, off the radar, wouldn't be enough for someone determined to silence her. One day someone or something would slip and then all hell would break loose.

From what he understood, turning Everett in messed with the money and plans of several high-level bad guys. Although he admired her integrity and courage, she'd put a nice bright target on her head that wouldn't fade anytime soon.

Looking around, Drew had to side with Casey

on this one. Although there was no connection between Addison and Mama Leonie's swamp home, it wasn't impossible to find this place. It might lack any evidence of civilization at first glance, but it wasn't far enough from the marked trails the professional guides used. Drew thought she was underestimating Everett as well as the local fascination with this place. He bent down, noting the size and shape of footprints that indicated children had been playing out here lately. That immediately vetoed his more lethal perimeter security options, but Drew's bigger concern remained: how long until her son encountered one or more of these kids and their seclusion was blown?

On top of all that, he knew Addison. She couldn't hide in the middle of nowhere forever. Her son needed an education, friends, community and support beyond the basics she could give him. She wasn't the sort to skimp on her values or priorities.

A breeze wafted through the treetops, sending them swaying. He checked his watch and swiftly reset a few "tells" so he'd know if anyone came this way.

When he'd completed the circuit, he grabbed the gear bag out of his boat and headed up the stairs to the shack once more. Reprieve over, it was time for round three. Maybe the third conversation would be the charm that convinced Addison to cooperate.

He walked in and set down his bag just inside the door. The kitchen, which a moment before had been full of happy conversation, went silent.

Addison forced a smile onto her face. "Right on time."

He nodded. "Perimeter is clear," he said.

"What's a perimeter?"

"We'll discuss it later," Addi replied, making a face that told Drew to shut up. "We held breakfast for you." She stood and crossed to the stove.

"You didn't have to." He wasn't sure what to do or where to go. He didn't want to sit down with the kid at the table, and there wasn't much room to help Addison with breakfast.

"We wanted to." She turned her attention to the griddle sizzling on the woodstove. "Drew, meet Andy. Andy, say hello to my friend Drew."

"Hello."

"Hi," Drew replied.

The kid looked at him, eyes narrow as he assessed Drew, then twisted around in his seat to look at Addison. "You said Nico was the only friend we had out here. You said everyone else was strangers."

"I didn't expect Drew to visit us out here."

What an understatement, he thought. "I didn't expect it, either," he added, bringing the kid's attention back to him. That day in the park, he hadn't gotten close enough, but now… "Where's your dad?"

"In heaven," Andy said.

Drew heard Addison drop something, but he kept his gaze on Andy.

"Mom says he watches over us."

"That's good. You know, I thought Craig Everett was your daddy."

"He was gonna be, but Mom said our plans got changed." Andy knew how to spit out the party line, but he obviously wasn't pleased about it. "I wanted a dad."

"Drew, would you like two eggs or three?" Addi asked, her tone overly bright as she changed the subject.

"Three," he replied, feeling happier than he should that this conversation made her uncomfortable.

"I timed you." Andy twisted his arm around to give Drew a good look at the watch. "Mom said to time you because I wanted to eat."

"That's a great watch." Drew admired the Captain America watch. "How long did you have to wait?"

"Nineteen minutes."

Drew gave an approving hum. "Thanks for being patient."

Addison put a platter of fresh pancakes on the

table along with a small pitcher of syrup. "Take it easy," she said to Andy. "Everyone will want some."

"Okay." He looked at Drew again. "My mom makes the best syrup."

"That's a good skill to have."

He watched, mesmerized by the kid as he carefully smeared melting butter over his short stack of pancakes. Then, sitting up on his knees, Andy grabbed the syrup pitcher and drizzled the warm, maple-scented liquid as if he were performing for a commercial.

"Easy," Addi reminded him. "Eggs are nearly done."

Andy put the pitcher back on the table and grabbed his fork to dig in.

"Impressive spread, considering the limitations."

"Mom is resourceful," Andy said, expressing the big word slowly around his mouthful of pancakes.

"Chew first," Addi reminded him without looking away from the stove. "And swallow."

Drew got up and propped open the door, letting some of the heat out of the small room. "Smells so good, you're likely to draw in some company."

"I've told you no one knows we're here."

"Nico does," Andy piped up. "Drew does."

"No one *else*," she clarified. "Mama Leonie didn't have neighbors out here."

"I don't know. People might follow their noses to this amazing breakfast," Drew said, taking the bowl piled high with seasoned scrambled eggs. "Is this dill?" He inhaled deeply when she nodded. "Can't wait." What did it mean that she'd made his favorite eggs?

"Me, neither." Immediately, Andy looked contrite. "May I have some, too, please?"

"Sure, squirt. There's enough here for everyone."

"I'm not a squirt."

"No offense meant." Drew sat down once more, the small table barely big enough for Addi to join them. "Do you have a nickname you like?"

The boy slid a glance at his mother, thoughtfully considering the question. Recognition slammed into Drew like a cold fist. He'd seen that particular furrow between the eyebrows on his father's face, caught the same expression on his own face more than once. The boy might've wanted to be called Godzilla for all Drew knew. The shock had created a sudden, loud buzzing in his ears, momentarily blocking out everything else.

The resemblance through the eyes was uncanny. This kid had the Bryant family eyes.

Drew's gut tied into a thousand knots. He couldn't believe it had taken him this long to see it.

The boy's father was in heaven. Or was supposed to be. Everett would've been a stepdad. Drew's mouth went dry, but he forced out the obvious question. "How old are you?"

"Almost eight."

As the math clicked, the savory bite of eggs in Drew's mouth turned to mushy cardboard. The fresh air and warm scents of the hearty breakfast soured in his stomach as the truth hit him like a body blow. He was looking at his son.

Good Lord, he had a *son*.

They had a son she'd never bothered to mention when she tried to give him the boot last night.

"Addison, can I speak with you?"

"May I," Andy corrected with a syrup-coated smile.

"May I," Drew said through gritted teeth.

"Right after breakfast." She didn't meet his gaze as she sat down and served herself.

"I don't think this should wait."

"I disagree. Go on and eat while it's still hot."

He set down the fork, unable to tolerate another bite.

"What's wrong?" Andy took a big gulp of milk and then dragged another bite of pancake through the river of syrup on his plate.

"Nothing." Drew tried to smile. "Just full up."

"Mom's a good cook."

"I've always thought so," Drew agreed. It wasn't the kid's fault his mother had lied to him his whole life. Technically, it wasn't her fault, either, though that line was blurred by the way she'd tried to get rid of him so quickly. Maybe, when this news had a chance to sink in, he'd stop blaming her for the emotions tearing through him.

Eight years. She'd been pregnant on their wedding day. When the hell had she planned on telling him? He wanted to believe he would've found a way to tell the army no if he'd known that detail, but in those days he'd boasted a bigger-than-life confidence. He probably would've taken the assignment anyway, knowing it had been a quick-strike plan.

Nothing quick about eight years, he thought. She'd gone through all of it alone. Pregnancy, childbirth, Andy's first steps, first word, first day of school. Her parents gone, her fiancé—the father of her child—presumed dead. She'd done it all without any family support. No wonder she thought she could manage this situation with Everett on her own.

His hands clenched. He wanted to put his fist through the face of the man who'd overseen his torture. He'd missed too much of their lives, but if he had his way, he wouldn't miss anything from this point forward.

He studied Addi, but she was focused on her food. "You talked to my dad before. When?" With so many questions in his head, he couldn't seem to get the words out in the right order to satisfy his curiosity.

"I'll explain everything after breakfast."

He didn't believe her. Even knowing it was irrational, he wanted to blame her for this overwhelming sense of loss. "I'm done eating," he snapped, pushing back from the table. Andy's eyes went wide and Drew felt the shame of scaring him. "Pardon me." He sat down again. "It's been a long few days."

"It's okay." Andy nodded with a wisdom beyond his years. "Did you have to drive forever in an old car, too?"

Drew looked to Addi for an interpretation.

She finally met his gaze. "I traded my car for something older for our summer adventure. Andy soon discovered how much we rely on modern conveniences like power windows."

"I'm done," Andy announced. "May I be excused, please?"

"Yes. Leave your dishes and go brush your teeth. We'll go exploring in a little bit."

He slid out of the chair, then walked over to

Drew and motioned him to lean down. "She lets you leave the table when you ask nice."

The advice, delivered in a serious whisper, had Drew grinning right along with his son. "Thanks for the tip."

ADDISON HELD HER BREATH, her heart thudding in her chest. The ornery grins on both faces were nearly identical. It made her ache for all the moments they'd never get back. She knew he was furious with her, the army, whoever else might have wrecked his mission. And after urging him to leave last night, she knew he had to be thinking she'd never planned to tell him the truth.

"Everett isn't his father."

"I've already said that." And by some miracle, she'd discovered Craig's true nature before he ever could be. "Andy liked him. Loved him like a dad," she admitted through the hurt and embarrassment. "He isn't happy with my change of plans."

"What did you tell him?"

She rubbed at the place where Craig's engagement ring had been. "You have to know this now?"

"I think I've waited long enough."

"Oh, please. That's bu— baloney," she corrected, glancing toward the bathroom. Appetite gone, she gathered dishes into a stack in front of her. "You walked back into my world less than twelve hours ago. Hardly a display of patience worthy of praise."

"You weren't going to tell me." His brown eyes were full of hurt and betrayal, but she refused to accept it as her sole responsibility.

"I told you plenty of times. You just weren't around to hear it."

"What the hell does that mean?"

"Watch your language." She glared at him. "And lower your voice. He doesn't need to hear us fighting."

"We wouldn't be fighting if you'd been honest with me."

"Like you've been so honest living in Detroit without so much as a note when you came home? I've never lied to you. I've never had the chance."

"What about last night?"

She shook her head. "I didn't lie."

"You sure didn't volunteer the information."

"I was in shock," she said in her defense. "The primary reason I let you stay last night was so we could talk about this today."

"Right." His glare would've sliced through steel, but she found herself equally infuriated with him. "When did you know?"

She knew what he was asking, but she made him clarify, just to buy herself a little time. "Know what?"

He stood up and in two strides he was towering over her. Pinned between his solid chest and the sturdy sink, she didn't feel the least bit threatened. No, her heart thrilled at his proximity and she inhaled his masculine scent. The woodstove had nothing on Drew when it came to creating heat.

"When did you know you were carrying my child?"

"Our wedding day." The memories came rushing back. With all the excitement of getting married, she'd barely had a moment to think about when and how she'd tell him. At the reception? Over strawberries and a single sip of champagne in the honeymoon suite? She remembered wanting to tell him before the morning sickness gave it away. "I did the test that morning."

Drew studied her, but she didn't know what he hoped to find. There was no reason for her to lie.

"I'm ready!" Andy came running in, shoes in one hand, ball cap in the other. "Can we show Drew the gator slide? Do you think the turtles will be out?"

Drew stepped back, his scowl vanishing as he knelt down to look Andy in the eye. "Have you seen any of the swamp by boat yet?"

"Uh-uh." Her son's eyes lit with excitement. "Mom said she'd teach me the boat later. Are you gonna take me out?"

Drew nodded. "If your mom says yes, I'll take you both out."

She had to fight the tears that threatened. How many times had she wished for this very thing? For Drew to see his amazing son, to be a part of Andy's life. Then she remembered what had brought him to their hiding place, what had dragged him away from his new life in Detroit. "Drew and I have a few things to talk about. Then we'll see if the boat is still an option." He'd been home for more than a year and hadn't so much as called to check on her. She wasn't about to hop in his boat and pretend nothing had gone wrong.

Andy's happy expression bottomed out. "You really mean it's not an option."

"No. I mean there's more to consider than a simple yes or no. Drew might have other things to do."

"Uh-huh." Deflated, Andy plopped down to put on his shoes. "Can we at least go see the gator slide?"

"Yes," she said with more enthusiasm than she felt. She turned to Drew. "Do you want to clean up first?"

"I think a gator slide takes priority."

She appreciated his understanding of Andy's impatience. "Let's head out, then."

Andy led the way down the steps and pointed out everything he'd learned about the swamp.

It seemed as though every sentence began with "Nico said" or "Mom told me." Thankfully, Drew seemed content to listen, giving Andy his full attention and giving her space to come to terms with this latest upheaval.

Walking through the quiet swamp beside Drew, the first and only man she'd loved with her whole self, was a miracle in itself. But how could she make him understand and bridge the gap between them, not knowing where his side began? And how would she ever explain to her son that his father had fallen back into their lives like an angel from heaven?

Andy gave a cheer when she agreed to let him climb a tree. Drew gave him a boost, then stepped back to watch.

"I'm not leaving you out here alone," he said for her ears only, his tone firm. "Everett won't stop searching. You're a liability to him."

"I took precautions."

"While that's great, it doesn't change anything. You need to trust me to bring you in safely."

If only it were that easy. "Stay and play body-guard if you have to. I understand why you feel you should, especially now, but I'm not going anywhere close to a government agency while Everett's loose."

"Then I hope Nico brought you enough sup-plies for three."

In all her fantasies of a real family vacation, Mama Leonie's swamp shack had never entered the equation. This was outrageous, yet, as she watched Drew advise Andy, as he encouraged their son, something about it felt absolutely right. It scared her nearly as much as it pleased her.

She reminded herself to stay firm. She couldn't allow the echo of her past feelings for Drew to color the tough decisions now. Thanks to time and circumstances, they were different people now. Even if she trusted that what she felt in this moment was real, she couldn't give in to emotions he might never return.

Chapter Seven

"What's a perm-a-meter?" Andy asked as Drew's footsteps faded down the steps and away from the shack.

Addison stirred the pot of gumbo simmering on the top of the stove. They'd eat as soon as Drew returned. "Perimeter." She waited while Andy practiced the word, praising him when he said it correctly. "A perimeter is an outline of an object or area. If you drew a line around the table, that would be the table's perimeter."

"Huh."

She nodded, smiling to herself. The whole day had been one question after another as Andy absorbed everything Drew said and did.

There were definite similarities, beyond the eyes and the fascination with comic books. Both Drew and Andy enjoyed exploring. From climbing the tree to watching fish ripple under the water of the swamp to spotting the various birds, they couldn't seem to get enough of their surroundings. Or each other.

"Why does Drew have to check it?"

So far, she'd only told him Drew was a friend, but she knew that wasn't going to satisfy her curious son for long. Or Drew. She dreaded bedtime when she couldn't use Andy as an excuse to avoid the hard conversation Drew was determined to have.

Why couldn't it be enough for him to know Andy was his? She didn't want to share her son. Anyone could look at Andy and know she'd been doing quite well as a single mom. Swiping the back of her hand across her forehead, she hated how childish that sounded.

Her emotions were twisted in agonizing clumps and she had no idea how to loosen them. There had to be a way through this mess so things could become smooth and familiar again. She took a deep breath. They were adults. Two reasonable people stuck in awkward circumstances. No one's fault, though a small, petty part of her wanted to blame him. If not him, then definitely the army, but that was a useless exercise that would only make her bitter.

Even as her wedding day fell apart, she'd understood why Drew had accepted the unexpected assignment. It made her feel like a horrible person to stand here wishing he'd stayed in Detroit. Not forgotten, but definitely part of her past.

Until this debacle with Craig, she'd done pretty

damn well. As a mom and as a corporate attorney. She didn't need Drew and his sense of duty and honor throwing another wrench in her life plan.

"Will Drew stay with us for the whole summer adventure?"

Addison feared that was exactly what would happen. "He'll be with us for a while. I'm not sure how long." It would be impossible to outrun him, but she hadn't yet given up on finding a way to make him leave.

"I like Drew."

"I'm glad. He's a good person," she added. It made her ache to hear how much her son wanted a father. She'd done her best to instill a sense of his father in Andy, to let him know his dad loved him, but she was discovering a memory—even a heroic one—was a poor substitute for the real thing.

"He watches you."

Addison's pulse skipped. "What do you mean?"

"When you aren't looking he stares at you."

"Well." She didn't know what to say. "He keeps an eye on you, too. As our friend, he wants to be sure neither of us gets hurt."

"By alligators."

She nodded, laughed a little. "That's right." But she needed to prepare him for the worst-case scenario.

"I'm too big to be alligator food." Andy puffed out his chest. "Drew said so."

How had she missed that conversation? Addison ruffled Andy's hair, seeing the baby he'd been despite how much he'd already grown up. She knew she'd never recover if anything happened to him. She braced for an irritable reaction. "While I agree with Drew, that's no reason to forget safety."

"Safety's why I won't be alligator food."

"Oh, that is good news."

"Can we eat?"

"Just as soon as Drew gets back." She checked her watch, thinking of the twenty-minute time limit. The bag was by the door, a black-duffel reminder that trouble could fall on their heads at any minute.

"We didn't wait for Craig to eat with us."

"Sure we did." At restaurants.

"Did not."

She aimed a raised eyebrow at Andy. "I know you're hungry, but—"

"Hungry isn't a reason to be rude," he finished, plopping his head on his hands. "I worked up an appetite."

That conversation she remembered. "We had quite an adventure today. What was your favorite part?"

"Climbing the tree. Next time I'll go higher."

Not if she had anything to say about it. "What did you see?"

"More trees, just like Drew said I would. But you and him looked really small from up there."

She smiled, giving the gumbo another stir. "I guess that's fair. You look pretty small from over here," she teased.

"Hey!" Andy said when the joke sank in. "I'm getting bigger every day. I'm almost eight."

"All right, big guy, get down three plates and set the table."

It all seemed so normal to set a table for the three of them. She checked her watch, hoping they wouldn't have to run before they had dinner. Her pulse rushed for a split second at the first sound of boots on the steps.

"It's me," Drew called before the second footfall.

Andy raced to the door and held it open. "Hurry up. I'm hungry."

"Andy," she scolded.

"It's true."

"You held dinner?" Drew walked in and gave the table a long look.

She nodded, tried to smile.

"Let me wash up."

She stepped back from the sink. The small shack had felt roomy enough when it was just her and Andy. With Drew, it felt cramped and she was too aware of him. Maybe they should eat out on the porch. It would be cooler than in here with the woodstove, but before she could suggest it, Drew and Andy were settled at the table.

"How's the perimeter?" Andy asked, taking his time with the new word.

Drew glanced up at her as she served the gumbo.

"A learning opportunity," she said.

"The perimeter is fine," Drew replied. "This smells great."

Addison didn't miss the immediate change of topic.

"Craig doesn't like gumbo, but you have to eat what you're served," Andy said.

"His loss," Drew said. "Your mom's gumbo is one of my favorite things."

"Really?" Andy's eyes went wide.

Drew nodded, filling his mouth with a big spoonful. When he'd swallowed, he set his spoon down and applauded. "Just like I remember. How'd you manage this out here?"

"Nico was determined to give his mother all the amenities, even if they're decades out of date and rough around the edges."

"She didn't have a summer house, did she?"

Addison peered at Drew, tamping down the swell of doubt. If he thought they were in immediate danger, they'd be on the move with that black duffel bag by the door.

"This is her summer place."

Drew's gaze roamed across the room, as if he were taking a visual inventory. "Should I save room for dessert?"

"We have some ice cream in the freezer outside."

"We do?" Andy stared at her. "You said we ate it all."

"I said we finished the chocolate. Nico brought more and I wanted to surprise you."

"Sneaky," Andy said with plenty of admiration.

It was the highest form of praise from her son these days. "Can we eat it outside?"

"We'll see," Drew replied.

Addison let it go. Though she felt he'd overstepped, she wasn't going to say anything with Andy watching them so closely.

"What does that mean?"

Drew paused, a bite of gumbo halfway to his mouth. "I meant it would depend on how things go."

"Huh. Okay. With most moms it means no."

"Are you an expert on moms?"

"Pretty much. Me and my friends talk."

Drew's eyebrows arched as he struggled to keep a straight face.

"When my mom says it, it means she wants

time to think so she won't have to change her mind later."

Drew's brown gaze locked with hers. "Good to know."

Addison managed to eat most of her portion of the gumbo while her son and his real father chattered about guy stuff. The reality slammed home, leaving her reeling. Given a choice, she would have all her nights just like this: a family dinner, aimless chatter, happy faces.

"Are you full? Mom?"

"Hmm?"

"You stopped eating," Drew said gently.

"Oh. I'm fine, thanks." She pushed her chair back from the table. "Who wants dessert?"

"I think I'd like to wait. Who's up for a boat ride?" Drew suggested.

"Tonight?"

"It could be fun."

She shook her head. "It's too close to dark."

Drew made a show of looking out the grimy front window. His big frame, so close, tempted her to touch. Years ago, it would've been her pleasure—and his—to reach out and kiss him, to take his hand, to share an embrace. Not now. She crossed back to the table, telling herself it was more safety precaution than retreat.

"We could do s'mores."

"In the boat?" Andy bounced on his seat.

"Not in the boat. Fire and boats aren't a good combination. But maybe we could find a spot and build a fire."

Now she knew he was up to something, or more accurately, she assumed he'd found something on the perimeter check. "Andy, go brush your teeth and get your things together."

"I'll brush after s'mores. Before bed…" His voice trailed off at her stern look. "Yes, ma'am."

Addison snatched the dishes off the table and carried them to the sink. "What did you find?"

"Trouble," he said. "Could be locals, or not."

"Then they followed *you*," she snapped. "Lead them away and we'll be fine." It was a lousy argument and they both knew it, but she wasn't going to just follow anyone blindly anymore. Not even Drew.

"You promised to let me do my bodyguard thing."

"Fine." She rolled her eyes as she took out her frustration and scrubbed the dishes. "You're sure we have to move?"

"As soon as possible."

"Where?"

"I'll find us something."

"Uh-huh. Put out the fire in the stove and let me call Nico."

"That's not smart."

She planted her hands on her hips. "Not smart

is wandering through the swamp at night without a destination. I'm making the call and we'll leave as soon as we clean up everything here."

"Addi, we need to go now."

"If there was time to eat, there's time to put this place to rights."

Together they had things almost done when Andy came out of the bedroom. "The toothpaste will ruin the s'mores," he complained, sticking out his tongue.

With a sigh, she stepped outside to radio Nico for suggestions on where they could go for the night.

DREW LOOKED AT his son, feeling a little less awkward with each conversation, but it was still strange knowing he'd missed everything up to this point.

"That toothpaste taste will fade by the time we find the perfect place to build a campfire," Drew said.

"How do you know what's the perfect place?"

"I'll tell you on the way."

"Why do we have to leave? I like it here."

"Me, too." Drew made a show of looking around. "It's pretty cool."

"It's a swamp fort. On stilts," Andy said.

"Should we make a bet on whether our next stop is on stilts, too?"

Andy frowned thoughtfully. "You can't put a campfire on stilts."

"Why not?"

"It wouldn't be camping."

"Ah." Drew dragged out the sound. "Good point," he noted. "What would it be?"

"Silly. If the campfire's on stilts, you can't reach it to roast marshmallows for s'mores."

Drew laughed. "You sure know a lot of stuff."

"Yes, I do."

Drew heard the porch creaking as Addi approached. "Did you get all your things out of the bedroom?" she asked her son.

"Most of it," Andy replied.

"Well, let's take it all, just in case."

"In case of what?"

"In case someone else needs to have an adventure here. It's not very big. They'll need room for their stuff."

"Okay," he grumbled.

They might as well take it all, Drew thought. Since she didn't seem to be in any hurry to cooperate with his advice. He gathered up the few items Addison had unpacked and put them in the small suitcase while Andy picked up the last of his possessions and stowed them in his backpack.

"Hey, what's that?" Drew asked, catching a glimpse of a familiar color scheme.

"My new Captain America comic book." Andy held it out. "Wanna see it?"

"Sure."

Drew sat on the bed, the mattress sagging, so Andy could watch him flip through the pages. "This is the new one."

"Uh-huh. I saved my allowance and Mom took me to get it. We read it every night."

"Is Captain America your favorite?"

Andy nodded. "Unless I'm mad."

"What do you read when you're mad?"

"Incredible Hulk!" He hopped off the bed and made a growling sound as he imitated the famous green monster pose. "Hulk, smash!"

"Wow. Remind me not to make you mad. You're scary."

Andy burst into a fit of giggles.

"Let's roll out," Drew suggested.

"Hey, that's from *Transformers*," Andy said.

"Sure is." Drew wanted to scoop up Andy and tell him the truth, but Addi insisted on waiting. It was all he could do to hold in the news until she was ready.

They returned to the kitchen, and Addison's pale face worried him. "Did Nico have any ideas?"

She set the radio on the small table. "Yes."

"And?"

"I'll tell you on the way."

He knew that face, knew it was all he'd get until she was ready to share. "We have everything from back there."

"Great. Thanks." She pulled a cooler out of the corner and packed a few supplies from the fridge.

"Come on, Andy." He held out his hand. "Let's you and me get the boat loaded and ready."

"Wait."

He turned, saw the debate play out across her features. Her pale blue eyes were clouded with worry. "Andy can help me with the cooler."

"That's a girl job," Andy protested.

"Since when is food a girl job?"

Drew came to his rescue. "I think Andy means we're in Transformer mode. I'll send him back up to help you with the cooler the second we're done with this load."

She shot him an assessing look so long that he nearly begged for her to give him an inch of trust.

"Drew?" Andy piped up. "It takes me longer than a second to get up the stairs. I timed it."

"Go on," Addi relented. "If you're Transformers, I can find my super strength."

"You're sure?" Drew hefted the bug-out bag onto his shoulder.

"The sooner we get going, the sooner we all get s'mores."

That was all Andy needed to hear as he yanked Drew toward the door.

Andy got a tremendous amount of glee out of the rubber boat Drew had used to reach the shack. But he surprised Drew when he asked about taking the boat his mom had brought along.

"What boat?" Drew had assumed, with no evidence to the contrary, that Addi's friend Nico had brought them out here and left with the only boat.

"Over here."

Andy trotted up the bank and pulled back a screen of leaves, revealing an old flat-bottomed boat with a fairly clean motor and a full canister of gas.

"Nice." He'd looked around in the daylight and walked right by it. When had Addi learned to do that? Maybe he was as useless as the army claimed. "We can take both."

"I'm riding with you."

Drew was flattered but refused to leave Addi out of that equation. "If your mother agrees."

The little shoulders rolled back, determined. "I'll ask nice."

"That's the best policy," Addi said with a little huff as she joined them on the wobbly dock. "What's the question?"

"If we take two boats, may I please ride with Drew?"

Drew held his breath while he waited for her answer, surprised at how much he wanted her to say yes.

"I suppose."

She didn't sound thrilled about it, but Andy's enthusiasm made up for any lack on his mother's part. Drew wondered if it meant she was trusting him, or if it was simply more expedient to agree. Of course, she had yet to reveal their next stop.

He knelt in front of Andy. "You'll have to sit still."

The boy's head bobbed up and down. "I will."

"And we'll need to be very quiet when we're on the water. Can you do that?"

Andy mimed locking his lips and throwing away the key.

Getting to his feet, Drew looked to Addi. "Lead the way."

They pushed the boats into the water and paddled quietly away from the bank. The motors weren't worth risking the unwanted attention.

Though she was only a few yards ahead of him, he could barely see Addi's boat and he followed her more by sound than sight. Weak moonlight shifted through the treetops and splashed across the black water. The mirrorlike surface shifted with ripples each time Addi's paddle dipped under, rose and dipped again.

Her years of city living and corporate success hadn't dimmed any of the skills she'd mastered in her youth. She was as at home out here as he remembered.

Moving through the night-covered swamp, with the subtle sounds of Addi's paddle ahead of him and Andy's soft breath behind him, his mind wandered back to the day he'd met her.

He'd come down to New Orleans with a few army buddies to celebrate Mardi Gras. Ready to party, he hadn't been ready to fall for the gorgeous blonde with the wide smile and pale blue eyes. Back then he didn't have a thought to spare for luck or destiny when his group of friends met up with hers in a blues bar in the French Quarter.

Over strong drinks and the sexy, low pulse of music, the soldier and the law student found some common ground despite their differences. Smart as a whip, only her soft Southern drawl gave away her Mississippi farm-girl roots.

He could still remember calling the next day, sweating as he wondered if she'd given him a bogus number and grinning like a fool when she'd eagerly accepted his invitation to lunch. From that moment, they'd been inseparable, holding hands, exchanging hot, breath-stealing kisses and longing for more of each other. By the end of the week, they were all but engaged, overlooking the tough romantic geography of her law school and his career keeping them apart.

That day, that first sweet memory and all the memories that followed had kept him going through every dark moment as a prisoner. His captors hadn't broken him because he'd had her in that sacred part of his mind, heart and soul. And while he'd had her, she'd had their son.

"You okay back there?" he asked, pitching his voice low.

"Yes," Andy whispered. "Is Mom okay?"

"She's doing great."

"How much longer?"

"No idea, but we'll have s'mores when we get there."

"Promise?" Andy asked around a yawn.

"I guarantee it." Drew balanced the paddle across his knees, listening. "Quiet for the rest of the way."

"'Kay," Andy whispered.

The swamp opened up and the sky above sparkled with starlight between the thick line of trees marching along the banks. It seemed the world held its breath, watching Addi guide her little boat around islands of cypress trees weeping with Spanish moss. He followed closely, keeping his boat on the same line as hers, unwilling to risk areas that might be too shallow.

They made it to the far side without any trouble and into another narrow waterway. At the slow pace, the only strain was on his patience, but he wanted to get far enough from the shack so he could determine the risk to her and Andy.

At last, she paddled for the shore, using a low-hanging limb to pull the boat in snugly. Her feet landed in the soft mud of the bank with a quiet smack and she had the boat out of the water before he could help. He had no idea what landmark she was using, but he was grateful to see the shadow of a smile on her face when they were all ashore, along with their gear.

"You really want to camp?" He had two tarps in the duffel.

"No. Our accommodations are just a short hike in."

He looked past her but couldn't make out anything but tall grass. Tipping his head toward Andy, he asked, "How short?"

"Five minutes," she answered. "You can time us," she said to Andy.

At just over four minutes per Andy's watch, Drew stared into what looked more like an abandoned survivalists' meeting place instead of a secluded spot to hide.

"This way," Addi said, adjusting her grip on

the cooler. She turned into the trees and led them across a narrow strip of firmer ground into a clearing. With her flashlight, she spotlighted the modest, solitary square shack with cypress trees as footers.

"That's a tree house," Andy said.

"Another of Nico's engineering marvels." She climbed the stairs and nudged open the door.

She turned on the light and illuminated a one-room cabin with a half-size refrigerator, a two-burner stove and a pot for coffee on the miserly counter. At the other end of the room, two bare twin-size mattresses were balanced on plywood and cinder blocks. He couldn't decide immediately which shack he preferred.

"It's the best option," she explained. "No one's used the camp for years."

"If you're sure." Drew didn't like being so far from the boats. As soon as they were settled he would go back and hide them. "I'll build that fire for s'mores." Uneasy, he renewed his commitment to convince her to cooperate with Casey.

Andy dropped his backpack on one of the beds and spun around, clearly the recipient of a second wind. "Can I help?"

"Sure. C'mon."

Once they'd settled in for the night and Andy was asleep, Drew knew she'd ask him what he'd found that prompted the move. He also knew she wouldn't like the answer. Although the hard evidence was circumstantial, his gut instinct said Craig Everett or his associates were steady on her trail.

Chapter Eight

Washington, DC, 8:10 p.m.

Director Casey's phone vibrated in his pocket. He hesitated to interrupt dinner with his wife, but with so much on the line he had to check.

"I know what I got myself into," Jo said. With her warm and wry smile she waved him off to take the call. "Go on and do your thing."

Standing, Thomas rounded the table, bent down and brushed his lips across her soft cheek. "These days are numbered, I promise," he whispered against her ear.

She only grinned at him as he made his way out of the dining room.

The display on his phone showed a missed call from Deputy Holt but no message. That likely meant they had problems on an operation.

Thomas returned the call, cautiously hopeful the news wouldn't be awful.

"I know you're at dinner," Emmett began, "but this couldn't wait."

"Fill me in," Thomas ordered, braced for the worst after hearing the gravity in his deputy's voice.

"Craig Everett was spotted near the University of Mississippi, but we couldn't drop a net over him in time."

"He's not even trying to hide his identity?"

"Not a bit."

In a case like this, a fugitive behaving as though he were untouchable increased the odds of serious complications. "We expected him to search for Addison. He must be hoping she reached out to someone there. We thought the same thing at first."

"Yes."

There was a "but" coming and Emmett's reluctance meant Thomas wouldn't like it.

"Our tech team recently discovered alterations in Addison's personal history," Emmett said.

Damn it. "Financial?"

"To start."

"Crap. He's working to discredit her if she ever testifies against him."

"She must know more than she's already shared."

That would be good for the case, but it meant Everett would do anything to silence her. Thomas couldn't help thinking about the latest school picture of Addison's son in the file. Drew had to get to her first.

"He's afraid," Thomas said, thinking out loud. "He must believe she's capable of eluding him."

"Agreed." A world of concern weighed down the single word.

"How far did our team get before they lost Bryant?"

Emmett laughed. "They lost him just outside DC. Picked up the GPS in the car we provided again near Oxford, Mississippi, but lost him on the highway south. We assumed he was aiming for New Orleans. That man hasn't lost a step, no matter what the army thinks."

Addison had a few childhood connections in the New Orleans area, though no one who'd heard from her recently. "Then he's still our best chance at saving Addison and her son, so we can use what she knows to take down Everett and whoever he's working with." Thomas prayed the fast and loose plan wouldn't blow up in their faces.

"Whoever the leak is on the inside," Emmett said, "he's covered his tracks with a damned cloaking device."

"That will make it all the more satisfying when we expose him," Thomas pointed out.

"True."

He appreciated Emmett's determination to see justice served to a traitor. "Drew will find her.

He'll bring her in." Thomas had to say it, if only as an affirmation.

"I took another hard look into Addison's life," Emmett said.

"What did we overlook?" If he'd dragged Bryant into this unnecessarily…

"Nothing, really. But she struck me as the sort to cover all contingencies."

"All right," Thomas agreed, curious now. Picking over the facts hadn't led them any closer to where she might be hiding. "That led you where?"

"Ole Miss law school is a pretty tight community. One of her classmates works for the FBI now."

Thomas didn't need the file in front of him to recall those details. "You think that friend lied in the interview to protect Addison? She said she hadn't heard from her."

"It might be a matter of not hearing from Addison *yet*. This woman is a hard-core overachiever. She doesn't leave anything to chance. It's one thing to send out the information authorities needed to make the arrest. But she's not stupid. She didn't blow the whistle on Everett without understanding all the implications."

"Keep going." They'd talked through this before he'd brought in Drew. What was Emmett leading up to?

"She has to recognize if not who, at least how

Everett was connected to his so-called investors. She sells her car and drops off the radar, but the big what-if is playing through her head the whole time."

"What if Everett wriggles off the hook," Thomas supplied.

"Right. The man knows her weakness is the little boy. Addison's a tiger, she's got something in place to make sure her son is safe and provided for if the worst happens."

"With Drew out of the picture, who would she trust with that kind of insurance?"

"I've reached out to a buddy at the FBI. He can check with Addison's friend. But I don't believe Everett would bother with the law school unless Addison mentioned someone there."

"She's got the family farm in Mississippi she inherited."

"Still no action there. Not even Bryant went through, as far as we can tell. I want to keep eyes on this law professor at Ole Miss. The file said he was supposed to give her away at the wedding."

"Another 'yet factor'?"

"If we're careful, I think we can ask again without tipping off Everett's connection."

"Don't put Addison's friends in jeopardy," Thomas warned. "We know that connection has significant access."

"Okay, I'll wait on that. One more thing," Emmett said. "About New Orleans."

Hope sparked in Thomas's chest. "Tell me it's good news."

"We lost Addison heading east from Arizona. Everett has been nosing around in Mississippi. Drew was last seen on the road to New Orleans. What if we set a trap Everett and his insider informant can't refuse?"

"Dicey." But he knew if it worked, Drew would be off the hook and Addison and her son would be safe. "We don't even know where she's hiding."

"No one does. That's exactly why it has potential. It gives us a chance to corner Everett with some discreetly placed bread crumbs."

Resigned, Thomas listened to the deputy director's idea, considered his available Specialists and gave his deputy the green light.

As he walked back into the dining room, Thomas felt the full weight of taking this chance. *Dicey* was an understatement, especially with the gross lack of real leads on Everett's government insider or even which department he served. But Emmett's daring plan, taking note of who responded and how, might be just what they needed to start peeling back the layers of the convoluted situation.

Chapter Nine

Louisiana bayou

From the elevated porch of Nico's sparse hunting cabin, Addison watched her son and his father build a small campfire. Small enough to avoid notice, she realized, wondering again what he'd found near Mama Leonie's shack. Drew showed Andy how to put the stones in a circle and the best way to stack kindling and wood so it would burn well.

Andy could've learned those same skills from her. She had in fact taken him camping in Northern California, but she recognized the differences. She could give her son the world, meet all his needs, but it wouldn't replace the father-son bond. Other men might step into the void occasionally as role models, but until now, she hadn't realized she'd given up on finding someone as good as Drew.

She put graham crackers and marshmallows

on a paper plate and then broke a chocolate bar into pieces, hoping they wouldn't melt before she got them out there. The small tasks helped keep her mind off why she'd come back to the bayou in the first place. Whatever Drew had found, it had to be a coincidence. She respected his precautions, but Craig couldn't possibly have discovered ties that weren't on paper, ties she'd never shared with him.

Her past wasn't something they'd ever talked about. Looking back, she couldn't tell if she'd withheld the details because it felt as if she was betraying Drew's memory or if she just didn't think Craig would find it interesting. What did that say about their relationship? That it hadn't been real, even in the beginning?

She carried the plate piled high with s'mores ingredients out to Drew and Andy, watching her son grin as Drew gave an overblown, in-depth lecture on the importance of finding just the right stick for roasting marshmallows.

Being a mom, she could see things would get messy in a hurry. She set the plate on the next to last step and went back inside for bottles of water and paper towels. It was hard to believe Nico managed to keep this place a secret, but she was grateful. Drew claimed he could protect them, but she wasn't ready to rely solely on him.

Craig had fooled her once. She wouldn't let anyone fool her again.

"We found chairs and we got a roasting stick for you, too!" Andy rushed forward. "Drew made it sharp."

"Thanks for the warning," she said to her son, avoiding eye contact with Drew.

They took places around the fire in folding metal lawn chairs that had seen better days. She wasn't sure she wanted to ask where they'd been stashed. Andy settled beside her, Drew across from them. She kept the supplies near her, just to make sure Andy didn't overindulge this close to bedtime. A few marshmallows went up in flames, but Drew shared his technique and Andy practiced until he could make them almost as well.

"This is a great summer," Andy said, his mouth full of his first successful s'more.

She couldn't argue. Indulging in the sweet, melting marshmallow, the gooey chocolate and the crisp graham cracker made her feel almost normal. The sensation was a welcome respite.

"Do you play any sports?" Drew asked her son.

"Soccer." Andy swiped a hand across his forehead, smearing it with dirt. "Mom says I can't play football yet, but I have friends who play already." He slid her a look.

She reached over and wiped his forehead before he could protest and squirm out of reach.

"It's the coaching style that troubles me," she explained. Her son was tenderhearted and when she'd overheard the deep voices and tough words at practices, it raised her concerns. "They're in an eight-and-under league. It should be more fun than work."

Drew shrugged. "Moms worry a lot," he said in a stage whisper, making Andy giggle.

"What about baseball?"

Andy sighed, gazing longingly at the plate of marshmallows. "I want to try."

"And you will." She hadn't forgotten Drew's stories of playing for his high school team in Detroit. More correctly, of his being a star on the high school team. Her plan to surprise Andy with a week at a baseball camp this summer had been ruined when she'd discovered Craig's horrible dealings.

"There's a community league that plays year-round. I thought I'd enroll him just after school resumes."

"Really?" Andy jumped up and threw his arms around her neck. "That would be awesome."

"I played baseball," Drew said.

Andy's arms slid away, his enthusiasm and a barrage of questions carrying him over to sit by Drew.

She listened, balancing a mix of awe and irritation as Drew and her son—*their* son—talked about baseball. She knew Andy watched ESPN, and in San Francisco there was always plenty of sports news, but she didn't realize he'd absorbed so much. It wasn't as if they made a family habit of catching the local games on television.

While they talked, she wondered if she'd really been as overprotective as Drew implied. He'd been nice about it and it had felt as though he was backing her up more than criticizing, but still.

She watched her enamored son hanging on every word Drew spoke. If they'd had a ball and a couple of gloves, she could see this conversation playing out over a game of catch on a sunny afternoon. The image made her breath catch and she reached for a bite of chocolate, letting it melt on her tongue while she tried to relax. Drew wasn't intruding. Whether Andy knew it or not, this was his dad. Drew wasn't the type of man to force himself where he wasn't wanted. At least, he hadn't been.

Whatever had happened to him after the army thought he'd been killed clearly had changed him. She was only sure of one thing right now. She wouldn't risk Andy's heart before she knew Drew's intentions.

"When the summer adventure is over, I'll take you to a ball game. A professional game."

"That would be the best!" Andy turned to her.

"Can I go?" He spun back to Drew. "Can Mom come with us?"

"Possibly," she replied with a calm she didn't feel. She didn't need Andy siding with Drew, though the hero worship had obviously set in. "Right now you need to go to bed. It's been a long day."

Andy's shoulders slumped, but he rallied quickly, knowing that sulking wouldn't help his case. "Okay. We're going exploring tomorrow, right?"

"Count on it," Drew said. "And you'll need a good night's sleep if you want to keep up with me."

Andy looked up at her, his eyes brimming with excitement that wasn't entirely fueled by sugar. "Can I—I mean, may I?"

"Of course you may sleep," she said, deliberately misunderstanding. Grinning, she added, "And yes. You may go exploring with Drew tomorrow."

Giving in was worth it for the sheer delight shining in Andy's eyes. They walked back into the cabin and she listened as he chattered on and on about riding in the boat with Drew.

"I like him, Mom."

"Mmm-hmm. I can tell."

"Do you like him?"

She couldn't lie to his earnest face. "Yes. He's a good friend."

"Will you come along when we go to the baseball game?"

Would she? Her heart and mind leaped to opposite conclusions. Of course she'd go, she thought, as would any protective mother with an ounce of sense. But her heart imagined how it would be, her son and his dad coming home and telling her all about their guy adventure.

"Mom?"

"We'll see how things go." It could be weeks or even months before she felt it was safe for Andy to be out in public. "First this adventure, then the next one."

"Okay. But I really want to go to a ball game with Drew." Andy wriggled into his sleeping bag on top of the bed. "He knows everything."

"He's had lots of experiences."

"Like this adventure is our experience?"

"Pretty much. You need to get some rest now. Which comic should we read?"

"Can Drew read it?"

The innocent request prickled along her skin like a poison ivy rash. She didn't want to share this precious time. She had, in fact, long since given up on the idea of sharing her son. Marriage to Craig would've been a partnership, but they'd had an understanding that she'd have the final say about issues involving Andy. Craig hadn't protested. Drew would make his opinions known even when she didn't want to hear them. "Maybe Drew can read tomorrow night."

"Okay."

Addison ignored the heavy dose of disappointment and picked up another issue of Captain America.

"I could read it," Andy said.

"Sure." She nudged him over to the other side of the bed, her back propped against the wall and her son tucked against her side.

"I meant by myself."

She checked her first reaction and forced herself to smile. "How about you read it to me? Then I'll be here to turn out the light when you're done."

Andy considered, his small fingers tracing the vibrant design on the cover. "Okay."

She listened and turned pages as needed until Andy's eyelids drooped and his voice faded. Satisfied he'd sleep through until morning, she walked back out to the fire to confront Drew.

He was leaning back in one of the ratty chairs they'd found, his long legs stretched out toward the fire and his fingers laced behind his head. For a moment with the firelight flickering across his features, the years fell away and she was walking toward the man of her dreams. But life hadn't been so kind. To either of them.

"You have to stop that," she said, halting before she got too close to him.

His eyebrows snapped together as if he'd forgotten where he was, who she was. "Stop what?"

"Stop promising my son things you can't deliver."

"*Our* son."

She *knew* it. Knew it would come down to that. It didn't matter that his claim was valid. "It's not my fault you haven't been involved," she said. He'd left her once in the name of duty, and when he'd had a chance to set things right he'd left her again.

"Cut me some slack," Drew said, pushing a hand through his hair. "Leaving that day wasn't my choice, Addi. Mad or not, you have to concede that much."

She didn't feel inclined to concede anything at all. "Let's keep the focus on the here and now, Drew. You can't get his hopes up."

"Why not?" He spread his hands wide. "It's clear he wants a dad. Good news all around. I *am* his dad. I want to make his every hope come true."

"And how will you explain where you've been all his life?"

He sat up and shook his head. "We will find

a way. Both of us. Together we can tell him so he understands."

"And so he accepts you." Why did that scare her so much?

"Is that such a bad thing? I intend to be a part of his life."

She hated the way her heart skipped at the image that popped into her mind. She could see it so easily, the three of them gathered around a dinner table or chowing down on hot dogs at a baseball game.

"From Detroit? You'll just pop in whenever it's convenient?"

"You know me better than that."

"I know the old you."

"I'm the same man." He sighed. "You could move closer to me. We could…"

She waited, but he didn't finish. "Are you in a good school district?"

"Probably not, but this swamp is hardly the pinnacle of academic power."

"This isn't a permanent relocation," she insisted. "Once Craig is back in custody, I'll find the right place to raise our son."

"If what little I've heard is any indication, you'll need protection. I can give you that."

She wanted to demand what he'd heard, what he thought he knew about Craig, but the day's events, the entire situation had caught up with

her. Pasting a smile on her face, she searched
for kind words. "Thank you for letting us stay
out here." Weary, she sat down on the other side
of the fading fire. It wasn't far enough away. "I
know you want to take us in, that you think Casey
can help, but I'm not ready to risk speaking with
anyone connected to the government right now."

"What didn't you tell them?"

She shook her head, thinking of the package
she'd sent to Professor Hastings. "It's better if
you don't know."

"I'm not so sure about that."

"You'll have to trust me, then."

He snorted. "That's a bit easier if you trust
me, too."

"I did trust you." Then and now, it seemed,
but she had no intention of admitting as much.
In her opinion, trust didn't have to mean giving
up control of the situation. She wasn't sure Drew
shared that opinion.

He came around to sit in the chair beside her.
As he leaned close, his scent and heat crowded
her. "Is that so?"

She nodded, unable to speak as her gaze drifted
to his mouth. She remembered his taste, the way
his lips had felt on hers. It was his taste, his expert touch that haunted her dreams and the recur-
ring nightmare that she'd never find anyone else
who could spark her passion. Had he changed,

had his kiss changed? Or would it be a reprise of the way it had been: an explosion of heat and desire at first contact?

She wasn't sure which outcome scared her more, but she didn't get the chance to find out. Drew leaned back abruptly and tipped his face to the night sky.

"Do you remember the wedding rehearsal?" As soon as the question was out, she wanted to snatch it back, but it was too late. The lid was blown off the proverbial box where she'd locked away her memories of that precious time.

"Of course I do," he replied, still watching the sky.

"We practiced the kiss." She couldn't believe how much she wanted to practice it again. Had she lost her mind on some belated sugar overdose?

"The minister looked surprised when I dipped you back."

"Your dad was worried we'd make it a Hollywood production." She saw his lips tip in a faint impression of a smile.

"He knew better. He loved you."

And she'd loved him. Even through her grief-stricken anger that his heart had given up before he'd met his grandson. She remembered feeling as though the army had snatched Drew away and stolen his father as collateral damage.

She and Andy hadn't been enough to carry Mr. Bryant through the oppressive grief and loss. It wasn't fair to even think it—then or now. She'd known better even then, but it had required many expensive hours of therapy purging those destructive feelings so she could be a better mom. Based on the grim emotions churning inside her now, she might have to book some more time on a psychiatrist's couch when this was over.

"I kissed you on our wedding day," Drew said.

"What?"

"And every day since."

"Are you hallucinating?"

He met her gaze once more. "Did you know the stars are brighter on the other side of the world?" He picked up her hand, ran his thumb unerringly over the place where her wedding band should have been.

He'd lost it. Something inside him had snapped. What was she supposed to do with a little boy and a mentally broken bodyguard?

"Every night, whether I could see the stars or not, I imagined kissing you at the front of that church."

She yanked her hand away. It was too painful to hear, to think about. Her emotions were a jumble in her belly. She feared what his words might mean, feared this desperate need to give in to her body's persistent desire for him.

She—they—had a son to consider. Andy's physical and emotional safety came first; it had to. "I'm going inside."

"You're running away."

"Don't you dare judge me for doing what I must to survive."

"Are we talking about the present or the past?"

"Push me, Drew! Go ahead and push me further and I'll prove how well I can hide. Even from you."

It was a struggle, but she held her ground when he came to his feet in a move as graceful and quiet as a predatory cat. "Push you? Addi, I know a little something about being pushed. I understand limits and the dark places beyond them more than any other man you know."

She'd only ever known him. Had never wanted to know another man. "We should've been married." Again, the words that came out were different than the words she'd meant to say. What was wrong with her? She needed space, time. And a different bodyguard. This was too much to tolerate.

"You have to tell Andy about me."

Oh, but she had. Without any facts, she'd told Andy about Drew as a hero, a patriot, a strong, vibrant man who loved him no matter how much time or distance separated them. When she'd learned Drew had been killed in action, her connection with their baby buoyed her through the darkest days of her grief. She'd named their son after his father. Wasn't that enough for him?

"I won't let him down. Trust me, Addi. Give me a chance and I won't let either of you down again."

She wanted to believe him. Her heart already did. His earnest expression cracked the wall she'd built up as protection from loss and pain. From the first moment they'd met, Drew had been able to breach those barriers, but she'd built them up again—thicker and stronger—when she'd lost her husband before she'd said her vows.

Mired in that grim place, she'd been so jealous of people who had family. Simple survival meant she'd had to build some sort of defense against the world or wallow in self-pity for being denied the priceless gift other people took for granted. Her parents both dead before she'd finished her bachelor's degree, she had no living relatives on either side of her family tree. No heritage beyond stories to pass to her son.

"I plotted ways to get even with you for leaving me at the altar. They were funny and silly at first. Romantic challenges, you might say. They turned darker as the anger set in when weeks passed and I didn't hear anything more from you." Why was she telling him this? It wouldn't change anything. "I kept the note you sent."

"Thank you."

"I named Andy after you, hoping the killed-in-action reports were wrong and you'd be happy when you finally came back." She reached for her necklace, slid the two charms across the chain. "But you didn't."

Standing face-to-face with him, she knew there would never be a wall or any defense measure capable of keeping him out of her heart and soul. She dropped the necklace back under her shirt and pushed her hands into her pockets. With Craig on the loose, she couldn't bear the thought of putting Drew in any more danger. Bad enough Craig knew her weak spot was Andy. If he thought for a moment she cared for Drew, he'd be a target, too. She suspected Drew would blow off her concerns, but that didn't lessen them. "It's too late for us," she whispered. "We'll tell Andy the truth about you. We'll figure out a custody arrangement."

"It can't be too late for us, Addi." He paused, clearing his throat. "What we have is—"

"Was." She cut him off. "Past tense. What we had is over. Our wedding and every day leading up to it are no more than lovely, idyllic memories for both of us." She turned for the cabin before the tears filling her eyes spilled down her cheeks. "Too much has changed."

"Not for me."

She didn't reply. Couldn't. Oh, she heard the words. They landed softly on her heart, following her to the cabin and into restless, impossible dreams.

Chapter Ten

The next afternoon, under a hot summer sun, Drew glanced across the picnic blanket, watching Andy help his mother unload their lunch. He was a good kid, and Drew couldn't fault how Addi had raised him. They needed to tell him the truth, let him adjust to the idea of having a real dad. It wouldn't be easy—for any of them—but that wasn't Drew's biggest problem.

No, Drew understood the biggest struggle of his life was with Addi. Whoever said love at first sight didn't exist didn't know squat about it. Seeing her, he'd felt something inside him opening like a key in a lock. Curious, he hadn't fought it, just followed, and soon he'd experienced a love beyond measure. A love that hadn't shriveled under the long-distance pressure of her law school or his busy military career.

He felt awkward admitting it, even knowing she wasn't romantically attached to anyone, but he loved her still. Desperately. It made him vulnerable personally and in his role as her protector. Temporary protector, if she had her way. He was afraid to ask if she might have any emotions left for him. The answer was obvious enough—she'd been engaged to another man. She might not be able to deny the old physical spark, but he wanted more than her body. He wanted her heart once more. He just couldn't be with her and not be *with* her. The physical chemistry was a good start, but it went so much deeper. For him anyway.

But this wasn't the time to navigate that particular minefield. They had more immediate problems, and any mistake could be their last. If he didn't get her into Casey's protection soon, if he messed up and something happened to her or Andy, this op would accomplish the one thing the POW experience hadn't: it would break him.

The time between their introduction and their wedding had been the best of his life. Before Addi, he'd had family, good friends and the best support a career soldier could want. But she'd brightened up all of that. Loving her, being loved by her, had brought all those pieces together. Loving her made him stronger, gave him something even more significant, more personal to fight for. It sounded clichéd even in his head, but it was true. Loving her, believing she still loved him, had saved his life in that hellhole.

He looked at Andy, then at her. Loving her,

he'd been willing to let her keep her new family and all the happiness he'd witnessed that day in the park. Now, knowing her son and their family of two was really his, he wanted it all, but he didn't know if he could give her what she needed in return.

Edgy and tense, she had reason to distrust the world, and if he admitted he'd tracked her down only to walk away, he'd give her a valid reason to distrust him.

"Aren't you hungry?"

He looked up as her shadow fell over him. "Famished." He didn't mean the food. Between their son and the imminent danger, he couldn't indulge his basic need to take and taste, to remind them both, on the most basic level, of what they'd once shared. She might not believe it was there, but he did. Instead, he decided right then and there to focus on what he could do. He could be the man he'd intended to be—her husband and a father—and he could keep them both safe until she trusted him enough to take her in to talk with Director Casey.

"Come on over and make a plate."

"I can't believe how well your friend stocked this place."

She smiled. "Based on that stash, I think he was planning an extended getaway. I feel a little guilty for taking advantage. I'll have to find a way to make it up to him."

"I like Nico's tree house," Andy said.

"Me, too," Drew agreed. Especially the wide porch that saved him from having to share the tight quarters with Addi through the night. "Has your mom taken you fishing yet?"

"Not ever," Andy said around a bite of ham sandwich.

"Chew first," Addi reminded him.

"I saw some fishing poles in that cubby under the cabin this morning. It would be a good way to spend some time this afternoon." Anything to create more breathing room. He couldn't decide if the temptation of being close to her was worse than the surge of grief whenever he thought of the time they'd lost. "If we can find some bait, we'll be set."

"What kind of stuff makes bait?"

He smiled at the boy. Drew wondered when it would stop feeling like a punch to the gut to look at his son. "The best bait is something that makes the fish curious enough to bite and get hooked. It could be a worm or a smaller fish. Some fishermen use fake bugs."

"Cool!"

"It all depends on what kind of fish you're trying to catch."

"Will you come, too?" Andy asked his mom.

Drew knew it was more than a good idea. Sticking together was necessary under the circumstances. At least if they were outside fishing, they couldn't keep arguing, and with Andy nearby, Drew would have a distraction from his perpetual need for Addi.

The three of them discussed the various fish living in the swamp and the different baits each fish preferred. Addi had looked perfectly content in the city with her fiancé and son, but out here she seemed equally at ease with her surroundings.

"You know, the best time to fish is early in the morning," she said. "Before the sun is up."

Andy's face sank with disappointment and his shoulders slumped. "Can't we practice today?"

"Definitely," she said. "But if you hope to catch anything, you should choose a cool and shady place."

The boy beamed once more. "Can it be just me and Drew?"

"Not this time," Drew answered before Addi had to be the bad guy. "But there will be other days when we can go out just the two of us." He met the hard look Addi aimed at him head-on. This wasn't a matter of overpromising. Come hell or high water, he would be a part of Andy's life from this point forward.

As they cleaned up the picnic and returned to the cabin for fishing poles and a bucket for bait, he kept an eye out for any sign of trouble. So far today, the only trouble was the prickly mother of his son. It was impossible to miss how they both used Andy as a shield, more than happy to talk to him but not each other.

He couldn't blame her, couldn't even imagine how difficult it must've been raising Andy alone. While they dug for worms he experienced a jolt of anger, like heat lightning, realizing how close he'd come to never knowing he had a son. Sure, he'd walked away in San Francisco, but she'd nearly pushed him away two nights ago.

It was a relief to head back toward the water, letting Andy's unending string of questions blur out the various levels of his worry and frustration. He taught his son how to cast a line, how to extricate the line from leaves and debris and then the more important lesson of sitting quietly while the bait did its work.

That last part proved the biggest challenge for the boy. Insects buzzed quietly out over the water and once in a while a fish would strike but not at their lines. Drew lay back on the grass, but Andy fidgeted.

"Who taught you to fish?" Andy twisted and knotted a bit of tall marsh grass.

"When I was growing up, my dad took me fishing on a lake that felt as big as an ocean," he answered quietly. "You couldn't see across to the other side."

"Where was that?"

"Michigan."

"We can almost see the Pacific Ocean from our house in San Francisco," Andy said. "But no one fishes there."

"What about on Fisherman's Wharf?"

Andy laughed, his small shoulders rounding as he tried to stay quiet. "No one fishes with poles and stuff out there. They get on boats and go way out from shore."

"Oh," Drew said. "That makes sense."

"How do you know about Fisherman's Wharf?"

"Stories and pictures. I've only been to San Francisco once." On the trip when he'd tracked down Addi and found her looking so perfect and happy with another man and this little boy. "California has a lot going for it. You must like it there."

"I live there," Andy said, as if that explained it all. "I learned the whole San Francisco history from school field trips."

"Impressive."

"And books."

"You like to read?"

"Yeah." Andy leaned out and checked his line. "Did that move?"

"Not the way we want it to."

"Oh." He slumped back, then shifted, flopping down to mirror Drew's position, propping himself on his hands. "Mom and I read every night."

"History books?" He slid a glance at Addi, but she didn't seem to be listening. "Those would sure put me to sleep."

"No." Andy giggled. "Comic books. They're better for bedtime."

"Which is your favorite?"

"Captain America!" Andy bounced to his knees, then remembering they were supposed to be quiet, whispered the answer once more.

"He's pretty tough," Drew agreed. At Andy's age, he'd been into comics, as well, and Captain America had topped the list.

He chanced another sideways look at Addi while the little guy chattered on and on about the story and art in the latest edition. At this rate they wouldn't catch anything, but Drew didn't care. The kid's enthusiasm was contagious. It had been nearly twenty years since he'd given any real thought to the complex universes and alternate realities of comic books.

He let his imagination drift, wondering what it would be like to have been a part of Andy's life from the beginning. He couldn't fathom a responsibility more rewarding than raising a family. A wife, a few kids, a dog…

"Do you have any pets?" he asked when Andy stopped long enough to catch a breath.

"Not right now. My hamster died."

"No dog?"

"Mom said maybe after the wedding." Andy sighed. "But now we're not getting married."

Drew managed not to wince at the reminder that Addi had nearly tied the knot with Craig Everett. The perfectly styled Everett didn't seem like the dog type, but Drew hadn't stuck around for a full evaluation. Maybe if he had done more digging, he could've saved Addi from her current predicament. Maybe.

He and Addi had talked about adopting a big hound dog, but that had been when their plan was to live on a small acreage. Instead, she lived in a city-locked urban high-rise. He stared out over the still water, wishing he could go back and do things differently. It seemed like a lot more than eight years ago when he and Addi had dreamed of life with lazy summer days tucked between demanding careers and raising three or four children.

He battled back the more familiar swell of angry regret over what he'd lost in that damned POW camp. The world didn't owe him a thing, but there were moments, like this one, when it was tempting to think so. He hadn't indulged in self-pity under the horrible conditions of his imprisonment, and this wasn't the time to start.

"Andy, if you had a dog, what would you name it?"

ADDISON COULDN'T HELP smiling as she listened to Drew and Andy. Only pieces of the conversation floated back to where she sat in a patch of sunshine, trying to forget her circumstances. But the few words and phrases were enough to let her know they were getting along well.

She'd been invited to cast a line with them and to enjoy the shade while they waited for something worthwhile to take the bait. But she was trying to show Drew she trusted him and meant to keep her word about making him a part of Andy's life.

Blame eight years of maternal logistics but she couldn't help wondering how they would make it work. She lived in San Francisco and Drew apparently had a life he enjoyed in Detroit. Just because they'd managed a long-distance romance ages ago didn't mean a long-distance family was doable.

Andy needed more than an occasional father figure. Now that it was possible, she wanted to give her son plenty of quality time with his real father. She suspected the relationship would benefit Drew as much as it would Andy. Not certain how it would affect her, she left herself out of the equation.

She rubbed a fist over her heart where it clattered against her ribs. In the early days after their postponed wedding, she'd had vivid dreams of Drew with the child she carried. Over the years, for the sake of her sanity, she'd let that fantasy go. Now, on this sultry summer afternoon, watching father and son, she felt it was a bit like being in the sweet bliss of those dreams again.

She shook it off, telling herself to stay practical. She'd raised Andy to know his dad loved him and had died on a mission, but she didn't know how to begin to explain this sudden shift of their reality. Andy was smart enough to know grown-ups made mistakes, but this qualified as a more serious error. Alongside her bad judgment in nearly marrying Craig and making that bastard Andy's stepfather, it would be a miracle if her son ever accepted her word on anything again.

How could one woman make so many wrong turns on such a carefully outlined path? No, she hadn't expected to be pregnant on her wedding day, but Drew would've been as thrilled as she had been. Losing him had changed everything, but she'd reworked the plan. She'd fled the Mississippi Delta and the haunting shadows of the memories they'd made for the West Coast and an urban life.

It had been the best option for her as a new lawyer, following the excellent money and perks that supported her as an unexpectedly single mother. She'd provided the best for Andy from his first nanny right up through his private schooling. She'd made a name for herself, rising swiftly to the top of her profession while staying involved as a parent and volunteer in Andy's activities. Sure, something had been missing—for both of them—but she'd done everything possible to compensate.

Andy popped up from the grass to check his line again, and this time Drew followed him. As she watched them deal with whatever had snagged the line, she understood there would be no compensating for the bond forming between them.

Andy idolized Drew already. Other than her fear of him promising things he couldn't deliver, she couldn't fault a single thing about how Drew interacted with their son. But she felt obligated to proceed with caution. It was up to her to protect Andy from the potential pain of losing his father again.

Drew might be her only ally right now, but there was no guarantee he'd stick around in the backwater of the bayous until the threats against her were completely neutralized. She'd blown the whistle on Craig, and he'd escaped custody once, confirming her worst fear. She didn't think he'd ever find her if she stayed off the grid out here, but she had to think of Andy's future.

"Mom, come look!" Her son raced up the bank, skidding to a stop beside her rickety chair. Grabbing her hand, he started to tug her to her feet. "Come on. We got a bite!"

"Way to go," she said. "You'd better help reel him in."

Andy stopped midstride, giving her a puzzled expression. "How do you know it's a boy fish?"

"Just an expression, honey," she said, waving him back down to the water's edge. If Drew wanted to step into dad shoes, she'd be happy to let him start with this topic. "Go check with Drew."

"Is it a boy fish?" Andy asked as Drew showed him the catch.

"This one is too young to tell," Drew said. He showed Andy how to remove the hook without hurting the fish. "I'm not sure fish care much about being boys or girls," he added, placing the fish in Andy's eager hands. "Be gentle," he instructed. "Toss him—it—back in."

"But fish have babies."

"Uh-huh," Drew replied warily.

Addison smiled, wondering how he liked parenting now.

"There has to be a boy and a girl to make babies," Andy declared, looking at each of them in turn. "We learned it in science." He held the squirming fish, looking it over from gills to tail. "Everything that makes babies has a boy and a girl."

"Well, this one is too small either way," Drew said. "Maybe we'll catch him—or her—again when he—or she—is older and we can tell for sure. But not if you don't put it back in the water."

Andy crouched, pushing his hands under and releasing the fish to streak away. "It's fast!"

"Being fast is the only way it'll survive to be a big fish," Drew said.

"Yeah," Andy agreed. He watched the water, his sandals squishing into the soft ground of the bank. "Can we swim?"

"Only if you're done fishing," Drew replied.

"Will we catch anything real big?"

"Not if we go swimming."

"Huh."

Addison took advantage of her son's need to process the options. "I'm going back to check on the sun tea I started." It was the best excuse to make a graceful exit. "If you catch something for dinner, let me know."

"Hey, Addi?" Drew's voice followed her up the bank. "Can you cook gator tail?"

"Please. If you catch it, I'll cook it," she tossed back over her shoulder before she could stop herself. What was she doing flirting with him? They'd had a similar exchange during their first long weekend together after they'd met. It seemed

Andy wasn't the only one all too ready to include Drew in their lives.

Determined to keep her distance and a firm hold on logic, she hurried back to the cabin, hoping he'd forgotten what she hadn't. As expected, the sun tea didn't need any attention. The water was turning a deep golden color as it brewed in the sunshine. When she spoke with Nico next time, she'd ask for some fresh lemons for lemonade. Andy would enjoy everything about that, including helping her make it.

She pushed her hands through her hair, lifting the heavy mass off her neck, letting the air cool her skin. With Andy well out of earshot, she found the radio and dialed in a news station, hoping to hear that Craig had been found and was back in federal custody. Would she feel safe enough to go back to civilization then? The answer wasn't clear. She suspected Craig had been dragged into this terrible operation by someone else, but she didn't have solid evidence to support the theory.

She changed the station, listened to a few reports on other situations, but hearing nothing helpful, she turned it off. What the hell had she been thinking? For the moment it was a grand summer adventure to wander the bayous, but that glow would fade soon enough. Andy would want to return to his friends and school. He'd want to play soccer and make sure she made good on her promise to let him try baseball.

Turning in Craig had been the only option, but she'd sure screwed up every aspect of her life in the process. Not to mention Andy's. The plan she'd been so sure about seemed increasingly rash with the hindsight of each new day. Hiding in a swamp didn't provide Andy with the social life and academic challenges he needed. How could she hope to manage indefinitely with nothing more than the barest essentials? He was growing up. He needed the structure and opportunities she'd originally put in place for him.

Maybe Drew was right. Maybe she should let him take her to this Casey person and ask for official protection. If she had someone to watch Andy… Taking a deep breath, she forced herself away from that fatalistic thinking. She was getting ahead of herself. There were weeks left of summer. Plenty of time for the authorities to unravel the material she'd provided about Craig's activities and make the world safe for her and her son again.

She'd created one hell of a mess and instead of resisting and resenting the one man who'd shown up to help her, she should show some gratitude. Assuming there wouldn't be fish, or gator, she opened the stocked cabinet and considered how to turn the supplies on hand into a dinner that would satisfy two big appetites.

Chapter Eleven

It didn't seem possible, but the mixed feelings followed Drew through the rest of the afternoon and into the evening. Getting to know his son, even if Andy didn't understand the real relationship yet, had been astounding. The kid wanted to know everything about everything. With every question, Drew fell a little more in love with Andy.

He thought the opposite might also be true, but he didn't dare ask Addi to confirm it. While he was trying to be respectful of her concerns and boundaries, he was eager for Andy to know the truth. Hell, he was an adult and he still ached knowing his dad was gone. From his perspective, it could only be a good thing for all of them if Andy knew he had a real father.

As she started nudging Andy through the bedtime routine, Drew offered to take care of the reading time.

She scowled. "Don't you have to check the perimeter or something?"

"I can read first," he pointed out.

She didn't look impressed by his suggestion, but Andy begged, adding big puppy-dog eyes to the drawn-out "please." Drew wasn't sure which of them was happier when she gave in.

"Just the comics," she said, shooting Andy a don't-mess-with-mom look where he waited on the bed.

It was impossible to mistake her meaning, and Drew fought the urge to argue. "Just the comics," he agreed. "Tonight."

He couldn't figure out why Addi was avoiding such an important conversation. Sure, Andy would have questions, but he'd also have two parents at his disposal to provide answers. She'd lost her own parents during college, a year or so before they'd met. She had firsthand experience with the gaping emptiness of losing a parent. Why couldn't she see her way clear to give her son a dad?

But she had almost done just that by nearly marrying Everett. She'd turned the bastard in, but Drew wondered how much she'd loved him.

"Turn the page," Andy prompted.

"Oh, right."

"I can wait if you're still looking at the pictures."

Drew had no idea what had happened to the story line. He quickly skimmed the panels. "No, I'm done."

"Okay." Andy didn't sound very convinced, but he turned the page and kept reading. "Do the sound effects," he said. "Please."

Drew complied, embracing the role with the same gusto his dad had used when Drew was a kid. He nearly burst with pride when Andy gave him a big thumbs-up when they finished. "Take it out to Mom, please? She'll want to know how it ends."

"You got it." Drew tucked Andy into his sleeping bag on top of the mattress. "We'll be just outside if you need us."

"'Kay," Andy said, yawning.

Drew turned out the light and eased the door closed as he stepped out onto the porch. He'd expected to see Addi, but the space was empty in both directions. For a moment, Drew panicked that she had been found and kidnapped.

"I'm over here." Her voice drifted up from the stairway.

He walked over, settled on the other end of the wide step and peered up at the sky. "Not the best place for stargazing." The view was blocked by the tall trees on this side of the cabin. He waited, but she didn't seem inclined to converse. In fact, she'd been a little too quiet all night long. "Dinner was excellent. Thank you."

"So you said. Again, you're welcome."

He searched for another neutral topic, but the

only thing he wanted to discuss was being honest with Andy or getting more details about her situation with Everett. "Was Andy born in Mississippi or California?"

She turned her head, giving him an expression he couldn't decipher. "Does it matter?"

"Not really. Did you, um, think about using my name on the birth certificate?"

Shaking her hair back from her face, she looked up at the treetops. "It should be a pretty moon tonight."

"Addi, come on. I have a right to know."

"I'm not ready for this, Drew. Not tonight."

"When?"

She blew out a sigh, clearly annoyed with him. "Just not tonight."

"You said—"

"You'll get your answers," she muttered. "Can we just enjoy the quiet for a while?"

In the past he'd had no problem sharing silences with her. Now, though, he could hear the clock ticking. Chalk it up to all his unexpected and unpleasant experiences, but he no longer counted on having time beyond the present moment. If she didn't want to talk, that was fine. But she could sure as hell listen.

"It was a three-quarter moon on our wedding day," he began. "I told myself I'd be back in the States making love to you by the full moon."

She didn't make a sound.

"No one ever explained to me how the mission was compromised," he said. "Could've been anything from intel to weather. Sometimes the people who claim to know guess wrong about who is working for which side over there."

"Over where?"

"The mission was Afghanistan. The prison camp was more like the fifth dimension of hell."

In the faint light bleeding through the doorway, he saw her catch her lower lip between her teeth. He wanted to kiss her, to soothe that spot with his lips. Imagining a negative reaction, he pulled his gaze away, focusing on the trees on the other side of the fire ring. It was a much safer view. For both of them.

"We went in as a team," he said, picking it apart one more time. Every time he went through those hours, he hoped to find an explanation. Maybe this time, telling her, would finally give him the insight. "A simple, straightforward graband-go kind of thing. We were ambushed on the way out. Our target got killed in the cross fire and two of us were hauled away to stand trial."

"By what authority?"

Of course the legal ramifications cut through her stoicism. He couldn't help laughing a little. "You know, at the time, I heard you say that very same thing in my head."

"You don't have to do this."

She said it softly, in a way that indicated she thought it would be painful for him. He bumped her knee with his. "Maybe I need to."

Her gaze rested on the place where their knees touched, and he assumed her silence was consent. Slowly, he cracked the lock on the door where he stored those awful memories, letting them out one at a time.

"The trial was a joke, obviously. They recorded me standing there in chains, listening to a long list of things I didn't do, spoken in a language I could hardly follow. Then they handed down whatever sentence fit their mood on that day."

"The army told us you were killed in action."

He wondered when and what she'd been told. "I'm sure the real story was buried under security clearances. I learned later that they staged my execution and sent my dog tags and the videos back to the army. It gave them free rein to do whatever they wanted with me after that."

Her shoulders slumped and her fingers toyed with the charms on her necklace.

He told himself she needed to know, needed to be aware that he could crack under the wrong pressure. Sure, he'd convinced himself, and her, that he could be her bodyguard, but there were chinks in the armor. The army had seen it first, forcing him into retirement. As much as he wanted to get Addi into Casey's protection, he recognized now that she was safer out here in the murky places of her past. A man like Everett didn't understand the nature or culture in the bayous. If Drew cracked out here, Addi and their son might still survive. Same went for a leak in the government that even Casey might not see coming.

"Emotionally it couldn't have been much different than what you probably went through." Only the night insects answered him. "You know, like the five stages of grief."

"I know them," she bit out.

"Right. So I was in denial that the capture was serious," he admitted. "Sure, it was obvious I was in trouble, but I didn't believe it would last. As a United States soldier I was sure someone would track me down and pull me out."

She slid those charms across the fine gold chain.

"Denial lasted me a good couple of weeks. I was trained to be patient, to look for the right opening. I knew they wouldn't leave me out there without good reason. So I did what I could to gather useful intel.

"My captors ignored me at first. They weren't what you'd call hospitable, but they didn't do anything obnoxious. I kept my mind on you. More denial, I suppose. In my head I was with you every day, imagining the perfect apology so you couldn't resist me."

"I'm sure I would've caved instantly, whatever you'd planned," she confessed.

Progress! Instead of a fist pump, he rubbed the scars on his knuckles. "They marched me across the mountains for a week, and while I was sure they'd taken another soldier that night, I never saw him. When we reached their camp, when I saw it was a prison, I went full-tilt pissed off. That held me for months, the anger during the day and dreaming about coming back to you at night. It even held me up when the torture started, but it wasn't long before I was bargaining."

Her face turned and the pale moonlight caressed her cheek. He wanted to touch, to feel the softness of her skin under his fingers, but he resisted. "I didn't bargain with them, just God, the army, the universe. We're trained for that crap, you know."

She shifted closer, by intent or reflex he didn't care. Their bodies brushed at shoulder and thigh and inside he rejoiced at her unspoken support.

"Movies and books tell you the reality is worse than the training. And everyone thinks they know how they'll deal with it. But until you're in it, you don't know there's something beyond the pain or the humiliation when your body gives in," he said. "The worst part is not knowing where the end of the line is."

She gave a little gasp but didn't interrupt him.

"It's impossible to underestimate the value of knowing there's a time limit for any given activity. June has thirty days and then July begins. If you hate June, you know there's an end, right?"

"Right," she whispered.

"There was none of that. It's all an untenable, unending hell. The food barely met the definition, and a body reacts before it adjusts." He laughed. "In the early days I complimented the food, saying it tasted like pork chops just to piss them off, to prove they couldn't break me."

"But they tried." She covered her mouth with her hand. "Sorry."

"Of course they tried," he agreed. "That was their job. Mine was to heal up and stay alive. They thought I had some valuable information about military installations, in their country or ours, I'm not sure. I heard them torturing other prisoners about the same stuff, but I didn't hear anyone give up anything you couldn't find on the internet."

"Impressive."

He snorted. "I suppose. I just don't think that crew understood the layers of protocol and firepower they'd face if they attacked." *Thank God,* he thought. "Every damn day that I could think clearly enough I bargained with the mud and air and the rats in my cell," he continued. "Just for it all to end. The shrinks say the depression gets mixed in, that the stages cycle through and repeat or something like that."

"Yeah, I heard the same thing."

Somehow, knowing she'd grieved, knowing she hadn't just left their wedding day relieved to be free of him made him feel better. Stupid, but true. "Acceptance," he said on a sigh. "I can't really pinpoint when that kicked in. Had to be after the first year. But accepting the situation gave me more days when I looked for a way out. In the cells we developed allies, identified the human rats planted to erode our flagging morale or to get information we wouldn't admit during the interrogations."

"Drew."

"That's existing as a POW." He knew she was fuming and it made him admit the rest. "Eventually you find a way out. It took me nearly six years before I finally managed to escape, but I was the only American that day. The only good news was, surviving the elements felt like a cakewalk after torture and interrogation."

"OH, DREW." ADDISON swallowed, grateful he hadn't gone into more detail about what he'd endured. The few scars she'd noticed on his hands and just under his collarbone were surely just a tiny preview. He was leaner than he'd been, and she suddenly wondered how long it had taken him to get back to this point. Six years of horrendous conditions compounded by nothing but pain and loss when he returned home. She couldn't imagine it. Admiration for his fortitude had her wishing she could ease just a small piece of his burden. "I'm so sorry." She covered his hands with hers, leaned in just a little more.

"You don't owe me an apology." He brushed his lips across her temple.

Countless times in his absence she'd missed that touch, that tender move that made her feel so cherished. She'd wished a thousand times that he'd walk back into her life, and now that he had done so, she'd made him feel unwelcome.

"How long have you been in the States?" She stroked her thumb across the back of his hand. Feeling the hard ridges of scars, she nearly wept for how he must've earned them.

"Two years give or take. I've spent most of that time in hospitals and rehab facilities."

"They should have called me." She gazed into his eyes, but his expression was hard to read in the night shadows. "*You* should have called me."

"I couldn't," he said, his gaze drifting to her lips. "I—I was too broken. You wouldn't have wanted to see me like that."

"Impossible." She shook her head. If he'd called, if she'd known, she would've been by his bedside in an instant, been with him through every step of his recovery.

"Even now, Addi—"

She silenced him with a kiss. A gentle, sweet touch of her lips against his. Barely more than a whisper, but she felt desire sizzle through her bloodstream.

"Addi," he murmured, brushing his thumb along her jaw. "You need to know I could still break. Some sounds, certain contact throws me off. If something happens—"

"It won't. I trust you." She kissed him again, lingering this time, enjoying the way her body remembered him.

"Hang on." He took her face in his hands, held her just out of reach. "Let me say it."

"Okay."

"If they find you and I…falter, promise me you'll run."

She couldn't stand the idea of leaving him to fight for the sole purpose of buying her time to escape. Not now. Her fingers curled around his hands, slid down his wrists. "I promise," she lied. He wouldn't listen to reason right now, and logical arguments were the last thing on her mind.

With his taste on her lips once more, need for him roared through her like an unquenchable craving. A need for him she thought long dead. "Seal it with a kiss?"

He hesitated so long she wondered if he'd forgotten all the *x*'s and *o*'s under the red lipstick print she'd added to her signature with every letter she'd sent him. Then, finally, with agonizing deliberation, he covered her mouth with his. His warm, firm lips washed away the tension she'd been carrying and her body went pliant.

Angling, she parted her lips and the first tentative stroke of his tongue had her moaning. He tasted of strong coffee and spices from dinner and the delightful, edgy temptation she remembered. Her pulse drummed in her ears. Here was the kiss, the passion she thought she was incapable of ever feeling again. She couldn't get close enough to his heat, his heart.

His whiskers rasped under her fingertips as she rediscovered the shape of him. Leaner, yes, but still Drew, the man she loved. Had never stopped loving. She wanted to tell him, but she knew he wouldn't believe her. She'd rather show him how nothing had changed.

She grinned as he pulled her across his lap, his hands sliding up the back of her thin tank top. Pressed against him from breast to core, his thighs hot and strong under hers, she felt complete, powerful. The danger of her present circumstances forgotten for the moment.

She kissed him deeply, reveling in the warm, sensual haze that had always come over her when she was with him. Only him.

His erection nudged at her through the denim shorts and she gripped his shoulders as she rocked against him. She moaned, the friction of the fabric between them deliciously unbearable. He made that familiar rumble of pleasure in his throat as she rocked again, sucking lightly on his tongue.

Being a single mom hadn't left her much time for dating, and her few experiences had never compared to Drew. She'd thought motherhood had killed her passion. Now she knew better. The most intimate parts of her—body and soul—wouldn't settle for anyone but him.

She dipped her head, trailing kisses along his hard jaw, down his throat and across the scar under his collarbone. His pulse raced under her mouth.

His hands covered her breasts through her shirt, thumbs bringing her nipples to hard peaks through the thin layers of her bra and tank top. Her head dropped back as she arched into his touch. She was tugging at the hem of his T-shirt, desperate to get it out of the way, when an owl called from a tree nearby. She jerked back, re-membering where they were and that their son was resting on the other side of a thin wall.

"We can't do this."

"What?" He stared up at her, his eyes glazed over, his breath quick.

She pushed against his shoulders, using every ounce of her willpower to scoot out of his reach. "This, Drew." She gulped in air. "This isn't the right time."

"Right time," he echoed, pushing a hand through his hair.

Suddenly she felt too exposed, as if the entirety of the swamp stood by, judging her. "We're outside." A lousy excuse and the wrong thing to say as his eyes locked with hers. Her cheeks flooded with heat when she realized they were both recalling a particularly erotic interlude during a weekend camping trip in a Mississippi state park.

"We'll go inside," he said, catching her hand.

"No." Only one of them was thinking clearly. She pulled free. Inside was worse than outside with Andy asleep in one of the two beds. She'd never had cause to explain a man in her bed to her son, and she wasn't about to start now. Remembering how it had been between her and Drew, she vowed that when they made love again—if things went that far—their son wouldn't be within hearing distance. "This—" she waved a hand between them "—has to wait."

"Okay." Drew pushed to his feet and moved

to the bottom of the steps. "I'll just do a perimeter check."

"Don't bother. We're safe," she said. "Everett doesn't know about my connections here."

But Drew left without another word. She watched him go, debating the wisdom of waiting outside for his return. Better, she decided, if she hurried in and pretended to be asleep when he got back.

Her legs were rubbery, her skin prickling with every sensation as she tried to settle down in bed. She needed the rest, but her body wanted the exciting promise of pleasure in Drew's arms. It shocked her, embarrassed her a little how much she'd wanted him. Needed him. One kiss and she'd blotted out all risk, all thought of his commitments as well as her own.

What did that mean for the future, assuming they survived Craig's inevitable efforts to find her? Her heart already had designs on reclaiming what they'd lost, but that wasn't practical.

Was it?

Exasperated with herself, she rolled to her side, putting her back to the door. She closed her eyes, but it was an exercise in futility until he came back.

Finally she heard him, deliberately clearing his throat and scraping the dirt from his boots on the top step. She placed her hand on the shotgun anyway until the door opened and she heard his voice.

"All clear," he murmured.

She didn't dare reply.

Chapter Twelve

Only when Drew heard Addi's breath even out did he let himself doze off. It didn't qualify as sleep, disturbed by the contrast of recalling her sweet body in his hands and the imminent danger he sensed closing in on them.

There'd been no sign near the markers he'd placed, but he felt the threat lurking in the shadows. Paranoia was a symptom of what he'd survived, and he struggled to keep his weaknesses at bay. Another move would cause more problems than it solved. Telling his body to stand down, he closed his eyes. With Addi a mere arm's length away, he couldn't stop wishing he'd done things differently.

If he'd escaped the prison sooner. If he'd just said no when the knock had sounded on his hotel room door. He thought of what she'd endured without any support and kicked himself for not grabbing the minister and insisting they exchange vows before the mission. She would've had access to his military benefits that way. He had known how to make the most of his available time and he'd squandered it.

In a twilight sleep he had that sweet dream of her walking down the aisle, but this time she wore a cotton tank top and denim shorts. It sounded just as miraculous when she said, "I do."

The floor squeaked, tearing him from the dream until he realized it was Addi rolling over.

What would it take to get her to open up about those years? He'd probably shared more with her than he should have, but in the moment he couldn't have stopped the tide of words. He finally understood what the shrinks meant about finding a confidant. Her reaction, those hot kisses, had been unexpected, filling the desolate places in his soul and smoothing out the raw edges.

He was dreaming of their first kiss as husband and wife. This time they were at the front of a small chapel with sunlight streaming through stained-glass windows. She wore a white gown worthy of a princess, and he'd just lifted her veil when he heard the slide and scrape of something near the cabin.

Awake once more, he held his breath, listening and counting the passing seconds. At the count of eleven, he heard the unmistakable sound of boots on the ground.

No time to waste wondering how they'd been found—it was time to go. With dead calm and absolute silence, he looked over to Addi. She was already sitting up, the shotgun across her knees. Good woman.

"I'll look," he whispered. They needed some idea of what they were up against. "Take the bag and wait with Andy."

She nodded, moving quietly to do as he said.

He headed for the door, leaving his pistol in the holster at his hip. Based on the sounds that had woken him, he assumed the boats had been spotted despite his efforts to conceal them. They'd have to push through the swamp and hope they found a safe place to hide. He intended to clear a path.

Wincing as the door hinges creaked, he dropped to one knee just outside the opening, braced for any reaction.

A silhouette rushed up the stairs, handgun raised. Clearly not a case of hunters or kids messing around. Adrenaline zipped along his nerves, bringing all his senses to high alert. Waiting for the perfect moment, he reached out and grabbed the black boot just before it hit the top step. Before the man could shout, Drew flipped him feet over head back down the steps.

In the commotion, he heard two more low voices check in by radio. A team of three. It made sense. Three men in a strike boat would be agile and mobile and feel confident about overpowering a scared mother and child. But were other teams searching other pockets and cabins in the swamp?

Only one way to find out.

Using the shadows, he eased back against the wall of the cabin, watching to see if the others showed themselves. A man passed under his position, heading for his pal at the bottom of the stairs. He heard the whispered comments and the call for reinforcements.

Damn.

Make a stand or run?

Run.

It was the best option. Out in the swamps they had the slight advantage of understanding the terrain. In the cabin, they were sitting ducks with limited ammunition. He crept back inside, hoping Addi didn't shoot him before he could get them out. He found her tucked between the beds, shotgun loaded and ready.

"Take the bag," he said. He scooped Andy into his arms. "Down the steps and bear right to the swamp. I'll follow you."

Eyes narrowed, she gave a short nod and opened the door. When they cleared the steps without incident, he felt a prickling at the back of his neck. It was too easy.

He paused behind the wide trunk of a live oak tree. "Stay behind me," he instructed.

Her eyes went wide and her lips parted on a protest, but he didn't have time to debate and discuss. He winced as his boots splashed into the shallow water, followed by hers.

Someone shouted, but they didn't heed the warning. A bullet whizzed by and he felt a moment's panic that the shooter had hit Addi. "Keep going," she said, putting a hand on his shoulder.

He did. Covering Andy's head with one hand, he moved as quietly and swiftly as he was able.

"Where we going?" Andy whispered sleepily.

"Some bad guys showed up."

"Really? Why?"

The excitement wasn't necessarily the best reaction, but it beat panic in Drew's opinion. "I'm not sure."

"Did you shoot 'em?"

"No."

"Are you gonna?"

"If I have to. I won't let them hurt you."

"I know that."

The little boy's certainty fueled Drew's determination and steadied him more than he would've thought possible.

"I can ride piggyback and you can shoot."

And the boy would be between them, better

protected. "All right, but you have to stay awake and stay quiet."

"I promise," he whispered.

They paused long enough for Drew to get Andy situated on his back. "Anything?"

Addi shook her head. "I heard them at first but not now."

"So far they aren't in front of us," Drew said, slowing the pace a bit.

"When the trees break, we should follow the inlet."

"Why?" he asked.

"Better cover."

She would know. He led the way as they alternated running with pauses to listen for any pursuit. Drew checked his watch as the first hour went by.

He halted their march when he caught the low rumble of an outboard motor on the water nearby. They froze, sinking back into the cover of tree trunks and bushes away from the shore. At his back Andy wriggled away from the tickling fronds of a fern, but the boy didn't make a sound. Thankfully, he didn't snap the offending stalks, which would leave a clear mark for those trailing them.

Addi touched his arm. "Do you—"

She stopped short when the motor died. Drew strained to hear anything helpful, but a radio crackled and his stomach knotted with dread when he realized they were caught between their pursuers and another team.

Damn it. Someone on the other side of the swamp must have spotted them. Given a rifle, with or without night-vision goggles, Drew would've made a more aggressive choice. Still, he had to do something to buy them a bit more time.

"Wait here." He settled Andy next to his mom and handed her his gun. "For backup." He set the timer on Andy's watch. "Start moving when that goes off. I'll catch up."

Any protest she might've launched died when they heard another radio exchange. This time on the shore. Too close. With a nod for Andy to start his watch, Drew slipped into the darkness and went to reduce the odds against them.

The moonlight drifted across the water as he crept along the shore. The boat, a dark rubber tactical vessel, floated just out of light. One man searched the shoreline with binoculars, while another remained seated near the motor. A third man kept his assault rifle ready, muttering instructions into his headset periodically.

Drew found a rock and tossed it out into the water, away from Addi and Andy's hiding place. The response was controlled, much as it had been when he'd tossed the man down the steps. A well-trained team of at least six.

Checking back with the team on the boat, he listened for any movement from the team trailing them. He was nearly on one of them before he realized it. Drew recovered from the surprise first, applying a choke hold. When the man slumped unconscious against a cypress tree, Drew relieved him of his weapons and radio. He listened to the comms as he circled wide of the place where Addi and Andy waited.

They should break any second now; the watch alarm and movement would cause another reaction, giving Drew better targets. It was the hardest thirty seconds of his life, but when they started moving, he used the stolen weapon and picked off the shooter on the boat, causing that team to run for cover. Then, like a snake coiled to strike, he waited for the last two men of the first team to come by.

When he caught up with Addi and Andy, they were making decent progress toward the inlet. "Just me," he called out, his voice sounding too loud in the night swamp.

She stopped and turned toward him, putting Andy behind her and raising the shotgun. "You're alone?"

"Yes."

Even in the mottled shadows of the dark swamp he could see her shoulders relax. "Good."

"It's a small window," he added, coming closer.

"We have to move quickly. There were two teams and I expect they have reinforcements."

ADDISON WATCHED AS he settled Andy on his back once more. She wanted to ask what he'd done, but she wouldn't do it in front of her son. Idolizing Captain America in the comics was one thing, but the finality of life and death in the real world was completely different.

"Did you get 'em all?" Andy whispered.

"No," Drew replied in kind. "Just the ones in my way."

"Huh."

"Quiet," she reminded her son. The night was far from over. "We'll stop soon." She hoped they made it to a place safe enough to give them time to develop a new plan.

Drew had offered to take her to safety, to tell her story to Casey, and she'd stubbornly refused. For good reason, she reminded herself as they progressed through the swamp. What she'd discovered about Craig made her skin crawl more than the idea of napping beside an alligator. As a corporate attorney, she had a basic understanding of international business law. As an intelligent person, she knew how to dive beneath headlines to see how world events would affect the interests of her clients.

"What day is it?" she asked, suddenly unable to remember.

Drew sidestepped a low-hanging branch, slid in some soft ground and caught his balance before he replied, "After midnight, so officially it's the eighth."

On the tenth, less than forty-eight hours away, if Professor Hastings didn't hear from her, he would go public with the additional information she'd compiled on Craig. The details included his bank records and his latest trips abroad. Surely someone, maybe the person who'd sent Drew to find her, could use that to see justice done.

As they followed the inlet deeper into the swamp, the muscles in her legs burned, her tennis shoes were soaked and squishy and the shotgun grew heavy in her arms. She wasn't ready to stop. Every splash of water, every call of an owl made her press on.

Another motor sounded, but this one was far distant and pitched differently than the attack boat.

"Not them," Drew confirmed, helping her over a fallen log. "Wrong sound."

She managed to get in another full breath. "Hiding in here gives us plenty of reaction time to any boats coming this way," she said, convincing herself.

"Down this inlet a boat's more likely to run aground," he agreed.

She jumped, belatedly recognizing the sound she'd heard as the soft scrabble and swish of an alligator sliding into the water.

"Let's stop here," Drew said.

"You should keep going," Addison said, gasping for air. "Andy's asleep on your shoulder. Keep heading that direction and you'll find someone to help you."

From one step to the next she'd hit the limit of her endurance, but she would not be the reason either Drew or her son died. Her arms and legs were scraped and scratched and she'd likely itch from a thousand insect bites by morning. All of which were trivial. "I've got enough shells to hold them off while you go."

"We'll camp here."

"Do we have a tent?" Andy asked, rubbing a fist across his eyes.

"Shh." She looked up at Drew, unable to make out his expression in the darkness. "Drew, you can keep going. I'll hold my own if they find me here. It's me Craig wants."

"I'm sure we've lost them," he replied in a tone that told her the discussion was over. She remembered that same tone when she'd pointed out the multiple pitfalls of a long-distance relationship.

She pulled together her fragmented attention,

another sign of exhaustion. Any argument would more likely reveal their position than change his mind. As much as she wanted to keep going, she didn't have any energy left. Besides, if the roles were reversed, she wouldn't leave him behind, either.

Saving her strength as well as her breath, she conceded, slipping the bag off her shoulder and letting it fall to the ground. The zipper sounded too loud against the backdrop of nature's night creatures. Biting her lip, she prayed the people after them weren't as familiar with the sounds of the swampy environment.

Taking in their position and the potential dangers from nature and man, they chose a place to create a sheltered hideout. Drew talked her through the process of laying out a tarp and settled Andy on it as soon as she was done. The excitement and escape had taken a toll on him and before long, he was curled on his side, sleeping deeply.

Together she and Drew cast camouflage netting between the trees. The humidity and temperatures had dropped with the night, and a light breeze stirred the air as they settled into their hideout.

"Get some sleep," Drew said. "I'll keep watch."

She stretched out next to Andy, the shotgun between her and Drew, but she couldn't relax.

"I'm sorry," she murmured at his bulky shadow. "What for?"

She trembled, grateful for the dark. His voice, pitched low so he wouldn't wake Andy or draw unwanted attention, lent a distracting intimacy to the moment. "Not going to see Casey when you first arrived."

He snorted. "How much does Everett know about your life out here?"

"Nothing." Just the mention of his name made her tremble. "My past wasn't something I talked about." Sharing anything about her humble life up to law school would've bored Craig. Sharing anything after she'd met and fallen in love with Drew had been too sacred for anyone but her son and therapist. "Seems I didn't know him well, either." She'd realized he had serious connections with too much information access, but she'd never thought he would hire a team to hunt her down. "At worst, I figured I'd be dodging private investigators for a while. Not…" She didn't want to call them mercenaries or assassins, but that left her searching for the right word. "Not anything like this."

"Something brought him close."

"It wasn't me." The words came out with more heat and accusation than she intended. "I didn't mean it was you," she added quickly. "But you're right. Something led him to look in this direction."

"It has to have been someone in town who saw you pass through."

Unfortunately, that was a safe bet. "Everyone has a price and Craig certainly has the money to meet it."

"What about Nico?"

Nico wouldn't have turned on her for any amount of money. "He's the closest thing I have to family." She sat up, drawing her knees to her chest and wrapping her hands around them.

"We'll make it, I promise. You should rest."

"I can't," she admitted. "I'm too wired." Too afraid one of those men would kill Drew or Andy to get to her. "Thank you for your help."

"If you really want to thank me, let me take you to a team who can fully protect you."

"How?" She wanted to hear he had the perfect escape plan, even as part of her cringed at the idea of leaving the swamp. Populated areas meant witnesses, security cameras and all the things that made it easier for Craig to track her down.

"I'm not without abilities," he muttered.

"You've proven that. Repeatedly," she said, scooting closer to him. His firm, sculpted shoulder turned to stone when she rested her palm there. "Without you, I'd be at Craig's mercy right now."

"How? What did… Forget it."

She sighed, assuming the question he couldn't

quite spit out. "What did I see in him? Right now, I feel like I must've been an idiot blinded by the polish and charm."

"You fell in love with polish and charm?"

"Hardly." She hadn't fallen in love at all, but how could she explain that without sounding heartless? "I'd known him a long time. Or thought I did," she amended. "Yes, the sophistication was one layer of the attraction."

Drew shifted away from her touch and she let her hand fall. It wasn't smart to get attached to Drew. She couldn't afford to entertain the idea of a future when she and her son might be on the run for a long time. *Our son,* she thought. Regardless of the short acquaintance, it was clear Drew was as invested in Andy as she was. Would he insist on serving as a bodyguard indefinitely?

Whatever had led Craig here, she knew she had to completely change things up if they were to escape. She had their passports and knew a few places abroad well enough to get started as an expat. The problem was Craig knew those places, too.

"What I need is a new identity. Know anyone who can create false IDs?"

"Of course." His tone was gruff. "But Everett won't let you anywhere near an international airport long enough to use them."

She knew he was right, though she wondered

if it would make a difference if she and Andy were traveling as a family of three. With Drew. Craig wouldn't be looking for that. The thought brought with it a flood of sweet images. Things she'd dreamed of and forgotten through her pregnancy and during the day-to-day details of raising a child alone.

Warming to the idea, she did the math. The money she'd tucked away would see three of them through for a few months. That would be long enough to develop a better plan if Craig continued to evade the authorities. She was about to suggest the family escape when his voice rumbled through the night.

"You won't have to run forever, Addi," Drew said, iron underscoring his words. "It won't come to that. I won't let it."

Another delicious tremor shivered through her. This man had a power over her that she'd never be able to overcome. Her desire was her problem and while her heart and body told her to never let him go, she couldn't know what he wanted or needed. Other than Andy. Whatever she and Drew would be to each other in the future, she would have to consider the father-son bond and relationship, as well.

"I'm too edgy," she said suddenly. "Why don't you rest and I'll keep watch?"

"Why don't you watch the water and I'll watch the trees?"

It felt like a manageable truce as they rested back-to-back. He was so solid, so confident, she felt a flutter of hope that he could get them out of this. He might call himself broken, but he sure didn't sound, feel or behave that way to her.

"Have I said thank you?" She couldn't recall precisely, but she didn't want him thinking she took any of his help for granted.

"Yes."

The swamp, unable to be truly silent, murmured around them for long minutes.

"Have I?"

She felt his words where their backs touched as much as she heard them. "Have you what?"

He reached back and, finding her hand, gave her a warm squeeze. "Said thank you?"

Chapter Thirteen

Her mouth dry, she could barely articulate a response. "For what?"

"For our son. He's—" Drew coughed "—he's amazing."

"He wants to be Captain America," she said, feeling her lips curve into a smile.

"There are easier careers than being a soldier."

"Life tosses crap at everyone, Drew."

"I know."

At her back she felt his shoulders rise and fall. He knew all the pitfalls and heartbreaks she'd faced before they'd met and fallen in love. The reverse was also true. She knew how his inherent need to serve and his sense of duty and honor had led to his army career. Those very qualities had drawn her to him like moth to flame and kept her heart tied up even when she hadn't realized it.

If Craig had his way, Addison might not have another chance to share Andy's early life with Drew. And if she ever convinced him to take

Andy to safety, he needed to know so he could better connect with their son. Not that she had any doubts about his ability on that score, just so she'd feel no regret if the worst happened. She trembled at the thought.

"Are you cold?"

"No." How could she be with him at her back? "It's summer."

"Come here." He shifted around, moving almost silently, until his back rested against a tree. Holding her hand, he pulled her next to him.

"What about keeping watch?"

"You can still see the water, right?"

"Right." She felt the grin spread across her face. So little had changed about him.

"I'm so sorry I missed our wedding."

His statement hit her like a sucker punch. It was the last thing she wanted to talk about.

"Me, too." Last night, when she'd told him she knew the stages of grief, she hadn't been exaggerating. Like him, she'd gone through each stage multiple times. The first time it was a mild thing, irritation mostly that the army had called her groom away. But when Drew's dad appeared at her door, holding out those dog tags... It clawed at her still, that dreadful feeling of being scraped raw.

Then denial, clinging to the strange mythical "sense" women often claimed that warned them of some terrible fate befalling a spouse or child. "Talk about denial," she said. "I extended the reservation at the hotel for a week, sure that you'd be right back."

He lifted her hands to his lips, kissing her knuckles. "I was sure of that, too."

"I believe you." She could almost hear the mortar crumbling as the wall she'd built up around her heart weakened more under his gentle assault. "I finally went back to the apartment and wandered through the local job offers."

"Anything exciting?"

"For the two of us starting out, sure."

"But?"

"When your dad came to the door and gave me the news…" Her voice trailed off as tears filled her eyes. She blinked them away, determined to hold up her side of the watch-keeping. "I had to get away from the things we'd planned."

"Of course you did."

His easy acceptance and understanding made her feel guilty all over again. "I moved to San Francisco during the second trimester."

"What were you thinking? You're a Southern girl."

She heard the humor in his voice and she chuckled. "I was thinking about schools, hospitals and providing for our son."

"You did good, baby." He wrapped an arm around her shoulders, pulled her in closer still.

She laid her hand on his thigh, slipping so easily into their old, tender habits. "Being pregnant got me through those early days." And her first round of real grief. Or was that the second? Both? Either way, while he'd been fighting to stay alive, she'd had something to live for. Their baby had become the sole purpose of taking the next breath, the next step forward while she waited for the pain of losing him to fade. Still, she'd gone through those stupid five phases again, twisted up with the typical hormonal and emotional turmoil after Andy's birth.

"When did you find out it was a boy?"

"On my first doctor's visit in the new city. I cried so hard and started calling him Andy immediately."

"You know I'd do anything to go back and change what happened. To be there for you through all that."

"I know." Addison sighed and pushed at her hair. "I believed it back then, when I thought you'd come back. And I believed you were an angel watching over us when they told me you'd died."

"And now?"

"I believe you want to be part of his life."

"Addi…"

She waited, but he didn't say anything more. "It's done, Drew," she said, hoping to bridge the gap at last. "Trust me, I never felt abandoned." God-awful lonely. Furious that life would demand so much. Often weary, shouldering the burden on her own, but never abandoned.

"How can you say that? I left you at the altar."

She felt her lips twitch. "You know very well I never actually got that far."

"Why didn't you use my last name for Andy? And you could've gone to the JAG office for support."

She'd thought about turning to the army's legal branch, especially for the benefits that could've been arranged for Drew's son. But after hearing Drew had died on a mission, she needed space from the military. She'd been fortunate enough at the time to find work that made that option possible. "He's Andrew Bryant Collins," she explained. "I wanted to honor you, for the sake of all three of us, but different last names as he went through school felt like more of a challenge than I wanted to tackle at the time."

"Fair enough." His chest rose and fell on a heavy sigh. "I look at him and think about all the things I've missed." He toyed with her hand. "Just when I get mad about being cheated, I feel guilty that you've had to do it all alone. I don't want you to be a single parent anymore."

Was he saying he wanted to be part of their future? Andy was nearly eight, but there were plenty of milestones left. At thirty-five, she still had time to expand their family with a brother or sister for Andy. It was all too easy to picture a quick, quiet wedding followed by the rest of their lives together. As a family.

The world didn't toss out second chances like this all the time. A silly, sweet proposal was dancing on the tip of her tongue, an echo of how he'd once proposed to her. The timing would be terrible or perfect, depending on his view of their circumstances. She just had to muster up the courage to ask him.

"Good Lord, Addi. Will you ever forgive me?"

She already had. "You couldn't prevent what happened that day and it seems like you're determined to make up for lost time now." She realized she was well on her way to forgiving him for hiding since his return, as well. "Following me through the bayous is above and beyond the call of duty for a former groom."

"Stop saying things like that," he grumbled. "It was supposed to be a few days. Two weeks, tops. Not the better part of eight years."

"And you should stop those kinds of comments." Six years of torture, deprivation and abuse while she'd had six years of first-world comforts, decent therapists and the company of their delightful son. Nothing could ever make that even out. "We both need to let go."

"Yeah." He rolled his shoulders as if he could shrug away the burdens she knew they were both carrying. "Do you have any pictures? From the wedding day," he added.

"Only a few of the setup, getting dressed, that kind of thing." Those snapshots were in the safe-deposit box, where she'd stowed them the following year, unable to look at them anymore. "Why?"

"I'd like to know if I was right."

"About what?"

"Thinking of you in your wedding dress walking down the aisle toward me kept me going. When I dreamed, it was of you. Any star in the sky got hit with my wish to see you again."

She swallowed and blinked away the sudden surge of tears.

"There were a few variations, but one dress was the default, I guess you'd call it," he said on a weary chuckle. "I said my vows countless times a day, determined to live long enough to say them to you."

He'd told her he'd imagined their day, but to this level of detail? It shouldn't be shocking because she'd felt much the same, but it was. Or maybe that was the chemistry zipping through her bloodstream making her feel so attuned to him. "What kind of dress did you imagine?"

"Strapless," he rumbled in a sexy growl. "White and strapless. You wore pearls."

She nodded. They'd discussed that once. She wanted to wear her mother's pearls when she married him. It had never occurred to her to wear those pearls to marry Craig.

"There was lace at the top," he continued. "Snug at the waist. I could feel the lace under my hands when I pulled you close for our first kiss as husband and wife."

Goodness. She wasn't sure she could remember how to breathe.

"The bottom skirt swept out and away in a short train, I guess you call it."

He had been pretty close to what she'd chosen. If she ever had a chance to marry this man, she promised herself that was the dress he would see.

"Am I close?"

"It sounds lovely."

"But am I close?"

"There was lace," she admitted. She was torn between affirming his fantasy and maintaining the element of surprise. Just in case. "When I get back to the city I'll show you the pictures."

"Okay."

He didn't sound too happy about the idea and she wondered which part turned him off. As she understood it, when he'd come home he'd basically hidden himself away. Maybe the old memories and obvious mutual attraction weren't enough to start over with. He wanted to be part of Andy's life, but maybe she'd changed too much. Maybe she couldn't live up to his memory of his Southern girl. "I heard you tell Andy you'd been to San Francisco once."

She felt the tension ripple through him. "Uh-huh."

"After, um, you got back."

"Yeah."

Would she have to pull out the story word by word? "When?"

"About ten months ago."

That would've been shortly after she'd accepted Craig's proposal. "Did you do any sightseeing?" she prompted when he didn't volunteer anything more.

"Like Fisherman's Wharf?" He fidgeted beside her. "No. I saw you with another man and a little boy. You were playing in a park near your condo. I watched for a little while."

Why hadn't she noticed him? She thought back, unable to pinpoint any day that stood out. Trips to the park happened too frequently. "Why didn't you say anything?" she demanded, anger spiking even though it was far too late.

"I couldn't." His voice cracked. "It was obvious you had a family, that you'd moved on. You were happy." He squeezed her hand. "I went back to the airport and waited for the next flight to Detroit."

Had she been happy? Happy enough, she supposed, with her healthy son, an excellent job and a considerate man who wanted to be her husband.

If Drew had walked up to them that day, what would she have done?

"I had to leave," he said. "No other choice."

"I disagree."

"You're allowed to do so."

She didn't appreciate the cold finality of that statement. "I had every right to know you were back. Alive."

"Did you? What would that have gained?"

"It would've gained you a son!"

"I didn't know that," he shot back.

Biting her lip, she held back the torrent of useless accusations and predictions. He'd come out, seen her happy and left. She tried to see it from his point of view, but she was too wrapped up in the pain as she imagined him walking away.

"You were *happy*," he repeated. "I couldn't mess that up. Sure, I'd wanted you to be happy with me, but I refused to be responsible for causing you trouble or making you miserable."

The pain in his voice was unbearable. "But walking away caused you pain."

"Not as much as you think."

"What?"

He sighed in the dark. "Seeing you happy and knowing one of us had found a good life helped me heal. It gave me hope and courage to make a life for myself."

"Oh." She had to wait for her heart to catch up with his words. "I wish you'd said something." When she thought of what he and Andy had missed—what she had missed—her heart broke all over again. For days lost and time wasted. If she'd gone to the JAG office with news of her pregnancy, would they have told her when he'd returned? She could wish and hope they might have at least told him he had a son.

"I understand, truly I do." Though she didn't believe she had enough courage and integrity to have done the same if the roles had been reversed. Guilt and tenderness and more love than she could hold rolled through her in waves. She turned away from the water, trying to make out his features in the weak moonlight. For too short a time this remarkable, heroic man had been hers. Always thinking of others first. Honorable. Strong. It was no wonder she'd never let another man close to her heart. Who could've measured up? She'd put him on a pedestal—for herself and

Andy—but she'd known even from day one that he wasn't perfect.

Just perfect for her.

She rose onto her knees and gifted him with a kiss. It was a poor reward for his remarkable courage, yet she put all her heart into it.

The moment spun out, the sweet contact quickly transforming into something hotter and deeper, stripping away the world until it was only the two of them. God, she'd missed this mesmerizing pull that made her feel weak and strong at the same time. Memories of this kind of passion had haunted her since she'd walked away from the church, alone and pregnant.

Reluctantly, she pulled back, her breath coming in small, shallow sips as she fought for control. Beside them, by some miracle, her son slept on.

"Take him, Drew," she whispered, sitting back on her heels.

He didn't answer and she worried she hadn't actually said the words aloud.

"Please," she begged. "It's the best solution. You can get Andy to safety. I'll deal with Craig and come find you."

DREW SHOOK HIS HEAD. "I'm not leaving you out here alone." He admired her courage, understood where it was coming from, but he refused to budge from her side. She'd never be alone again if he had any choice in the matter.

"You could keep him safe in Detroit," she pleaded. "Craig doesn't know anything about you."

"No, Addi. We'll get through this together." He turned her so her back rested against his chest while he used the tree for support. Her legs were pale, bracketed by his, and their hands linked lightly across her waist. In the quiet, he thought she might sleep, but soon she was toying with the charms on her necklace, a sure sign her brain was still working overtime.

"What's that?" He couldn't quite squelch the jealousy, wondering who'd given her something she valued so much.

She tensed. "You heard something?"

"Relax. I was asking about the necklace. You didn't wear anything like that—"

"When we were together," she finished for him.

"Exactly." It felt so natural to hear her do that again. They'd often finished each other's sentences or train of thought. He'd been curious about the necklace since he'd noticed it that first night at Mama Leonie's shack, but he wasn't sure he could cope if the answer involved Everett.

Now, after hearing everything she'd never shared with Everett, he suspected she'd never loved the man. Which gave him hope that the bastard had nothing to do with the necklace. She wasn't wearing an engagement ring, either. Not even the one he'd given her.

He waited while she fidgeted, watching her rub one toe up and down her opposite calf. Bug bites or nerves? Likely a bit of both. He knew she wouldn't lie to him, but somehow it made him feel better that she didn't just offer up a quick answer.

"You remember that necklace you gave me for our three-month anniversary?"

He'd never forgotten the little heart-shaped charm inscribed with their initials and the date they'd met. "You rarely wore it."

"That's not true." She made a little noise of impatience. "I just bought a longer chain and you know it."

"Maybe," he teased. He remembered that she didn't like anything right up close to her throat. Except his lips. The thought, the memories of having her in his arms, under him, sighing his name made him hard. Not the time or place, but he promised himself he wouldn't leave her, and he definitely wouldn't let her resume her old life before they had a chance to rediscover the explosive chemistry between them.

"Between the necklace and the engagement

ring you gave me, I felt loved and safe. Weird, but true."

It didn't sound weird at all to him. "In my cell, I used to think about holding hands with you, remembering how your ring felt between my fingers."

"Drew."

The way she sighed his name had his whole body aching to claim hers.

"That charm felt like my anchor. A talisman. I nearly panicked when that little diamond came loose one day."

"Did you find it?"

"Yes, through a fit of tears," she said. "A jeweler reset it for me, but I worried about it anyway." She took a breath and held it. "When your dad told me the awful news, he gave me your dog tags."

"What?" A chill raised the hair at the back of his neck. He couldn't quite picture his father doing something like that.

"For the baby," she explained. "He stood at my door and told me the chaplain had delivered the news. He couldn't bring himself to do a formal memorial service, but he wanted me to have something to show our child.

"When he left, I slipped them over my head and wore them alongside the necklace through the rest of my pregnancy," she whispered in a raw voice. "And the delivery, too, so it felt like you were there with us."

He stroked her shoulders. Speaking was impossible.

"I'd had to take off the engagement ring during my last trimester. I slid it onto the same chain with your tags. On the day that would've been our first wedding anniversary, I decided to set the tags aside for Andy, but I had the jeweler make these charms first." She held them up, even though it was too dark for him to see. "One is a miniature of your dog tag and the other is the heart charm, but I had the date changed to Andy's birthday."

Same initials, only a slightly different meaning. Was it any wonder he loved her? "What about the engagement ring?"

"It's in a safe-deposit box waiting for the day when Andy wants to propose. I thought you'd appreciate giving him that option."

"You were right." Her thoughtfulness, her care for preserving the best of what they'd had only proved how right they'd been for each other. He'd been so lucky to find her. Would he be lucky enough to keep her?

"When Andy was four, I showed him your dog tags and really started explaining who you were. Andy has them still." She twisted around, frowning. "Unless they were left behind at Nico's cabin."

He hoped not, for Andy's sake. He kissed her right on that crease between her eyebrows. "We'll go back and look if he doesn't have them." Drew had been motivated to protect Addi and wrap up this mess before, but he was doubly motivated now.

In the bag he'd packed two transmitters that would call in Casey's reinforcements. It was tempting to activate one right now and get the hell out of here, but it would potentially give Everett room to escape again. If Everett thought he'd lost all hope of stopping Addi, he would surely disappear.

When they left this swamp, Drew wanted to be sure they wouldn't be looking over their shoulders for danger the rest of their lives. Besides, Addi wouldn't rest until justice had been served to Everett.

So close. The moment that was accomplished, sooner if it proved necessary, Drew would hit his knees and beg for her to take him back. He could practically smell what life would be like with her. Waking up each morning next to the woman he loved as their son slept in his bedroom down the hall. He could hear the patter of small feet as they filled a house with children. He wanted to see her pregnant, experience every minute of that with her, if she was willing.

He stroked his hands up and down her arms,

just needing the contact. She'd worn his dog tags in one way or another since he'd disappeared. Surely a shrink would agree that it symbolized a commitment of some sort. He wanted to believe, like him, she'd never given up on the dreams they'd shared.

He cringed as she went back to watching the water. They were out here partly because of him, and she deserved his best to overcome it. If by some cruel twist of fate Everett got the better of them, he knew a shrink wouldn't be enough for him to recover. He just couldn't lose her again. "Addi?"

"Hmm?"

"If I'd come forward that day in the park, would you have taken me back?"

"The minute I'd been revived from fainting."

That scenario was laughable. "I don't think so. You didn't faint when I found you in the swamp."

"I was in mama-bear mode and not about to let anything near my son. *Our* son."

Her correction was sobering. "I'm sorry I didn't come forward. You might not be in this mess if I had."

His skin sizzled when she rubbed a hand along his thigh. "I'll grant this isn't ideal, but I choose to believe we're right where we should be. The lost time is unfortunate, but I hate to think how long Everett would've gotten away with his illegal deals if I hadn't recognized something was off."

"There is that," he agreed.

They seemed to be out of words again and a companionable silence fell over them as they kept watch. He thought she might've dozed as her head rested on his chest, but it didn't matter. He was alert enough for both of them.

Once more he considered activating a transmitter, and then rejected the idea yet again. He'd use both of them, but not until he could put one of them on Everett.

"Drew?"

"Yeah."

"In the morning I want us to tell Andy the truth."

"About me?" The silk of her hair brushed his arm as she nodded. He swallowed. "Okay." He had no idea how she'd start that conversation, but he'd happily back her up.

"Then I want you to take us to Casey."

"If you're sure."

"I'm sure we've wasted enough time and energy with this game of cat and mouse. I'd rather get back on the offensive."

He was all for that. "What changed your mind?"

"Having you as an ally."

As an answer, he felt that was a good start.

"Then that's what we'll do." He pressed a kiss to the top of her head and tried not to think about what she would do when the threat was eliminated and she had the world at her feet again.

Whatever happened, he wanted her to know one option was to reunite as a family.

Chapter Fourteen

Having never drifted into a sound sleep, Addison came fully awake at the sound of a boat running aground downstream. The black water of the swamps disguised all kinds of debris that frequently tangled up motor blades and dented or cracked hulls. Sunken logs, inexplicably changing depths, root systems and animal habitats all combined to make the swamps an ever-changing environment. Navigating the area was less about maps and direction and more about knowing what to watch for along the way. It had all seemed to come back to her, like riding a bike, since she'd arrived.

The sudden outburst of angry voices and resulting commotion made it a safe bet the frustrated boaters were likely part of the team hunting her. Why couldn't they shake them? The rising sun put a glow behind the trees to the east, but there were shadows still working in their favor.

They needed to decide on the fastest route to rendezvous with Drew's friend Casey.

With her hand on her shotgun, she looked to Andy. Drew was already there, waking him gently and urging him to be quiet.

"Mom," he whispered, tugging on her free hand. His eyes were wide and a little desperate. At first she thought it was the situation, but then she realized he had to pee. The very normal need made her smile. In as calm a voice as she could muster, she let him know where to relieve himself.

She exchanged a look with Drew and knew telling their son he had two parents would have to wait, not just for nature's call, but until they could speak without fear of capture. When Andy was ready, she looked to Drew. "Which way?"

"We're pinned between two teams."

Panic threatened, but she kept her gaze on him. "What do you mean?"

Drew raised his chin in the direction of the trees. "A team went by about two hours ago and again half an hour ago in the other direction."

"Are they lost?" she asked hopefully.

"I don't think we're that lucky."

Damn. She calculated the choices. It would be so easy to trudge up the swamp and let Everett's men haul her in. The move sounded foolish, but she felt it would give her back some control, especially if Drew used the time to get away with Andy.

The words were on her lips, but Drew was already shaking his head. "Don't you even think about it. We'll do this together."

"Fine." The odds were stacking up against them anyway, and working together was better than struggling alone, she had to admit.

Although hiding deep along the inlet had given them better protection through the night, now they were stuck. Drew boosted Andy onto his back again while she slipped the bag across her body and checked the load on the shotgun. They didn't risk the noise or movement of tearing down their shelter. "Your call," she said. "I'll follow you."

His brown eyes held hers for a long moment as he silently confirmed her full meaning.

She wished he'd hurry up and start moving. At this point the direction didn't matter; she just wanted to get on with it. Standing here waiting to be discovered was making her antsy. She didn't know exactly what he had planned, only that she trusted him to make the right call. For all of them.

"We'll circle back to Nico's cabin."

She nodded. If the radio was still there, if the boats were intact, they had better options.

They set out at a brisk pace and soon crossed the broken twigs and stomped undergrowth from where the other team had been wandering through the night. It wasn't the ideal family hike and she gave a start when Andy asked about fishing.

She held a finger to her lips.

"But it's early. The fish will be biting."

"Another time, I promise," Drew said, cutting short the protest.

"I can walk," Andy started again a few minutes later.

"I'll let you prove it later," Drew answered.

"Promise?"

"Yes."

"'Kay."

Addison shook her head at the two of them as she fell into step behind Drew. His long legs made quick work as he marched along in the fresh tracks left by the others. No point asking why; she was sure he had good reason for taking this route. It was certainly easier walking in areas already torn up by people who didn't care about leaving a trail.

The voices from the boat faded, but the occasional attempts to restart the motor cut through the natural morning sounds of the swamp, jarring her every time. A shout from behind had her turning and she caught movement from the direction of their inlet camp.

"We've been spotted."

Drew shifted gears, his long legs creating distance. She jogged behind him, hitting the dirt when a gunshot sent a flock of birds into the air.

"Run!" Drew put Andy down, placed their son's hand in hers and sent them on, turning back to deal with the attack.

She ran as fast as Andy could go, sliding into the only cover as soon as she spotted a knot of bushes. Sinking to her knees in mud, she propped Andy on her hip. "Tell me if someone comes up behind me."

She waited, willing Drew to join them. She wouldn't let him change the definition of *together* now. He jogged into view moments later and offered her a hand out of the muck.

"They're trying to flush us out," he said as another bullet bit into a tree well above their heads. "Either they've never used those guns, or they want you alive."

It wasn't much relief and she had no confidence that Everett's orders would leave Andy and Drew alive, too.

"Too bad. I don't want them at all."

His smile was edgy and dangerous. "Then we'd best hurry."

THEY REACHED THE tree line near Nico's cabin and skidded to a stop. Drew was surprised it was still standing. He'd expected them to have burned it to the ground, eliminating Addi's options. He didn't see any activity and the place appeared deserted, but the fire pit had been used recently. Probably this morning, he thought, catching the faint scent of wood smoke in the air.

Only a short hike between them and the boats they'd left. Everett's men would be on them any minute, and if they didn't move now, it would be open season on Addi. "We'll go for the boats." And deal with it later if they were no good.

They made it across the clearing and through the marsh grass and trees to the far shore. Spotting the boats they'd pulled onto the shore, he stopped, assessing the area for any threat. It was the perfect spot for an ambush. If he only knew how many they were up against.

"That's Nico's boat." Andy pointed.

"Right." But Drew's boat, the faster of the two they'd brought, was missing. Drew knew Addi trusted the old man, but if Everett had turned him, it explained how they'd been found.

"Craig doesn't know anything about Nico or his mother."

"You're sure?"

"Yes," she said through clenched teeth. "The water is our best hope to escape."

Knowing she was right didn't make it any easier to race across the open space, into what could easily be a trap. He was surprised when no one rushed from the shore or the water to intercept them.

Beyond a quick prayer of gratitude, Drew didn't waste any thought on their good fortune. At first glance, both Addi's and Nico's boats looked to be in good condition.

"Help your mom," Drew said to Andy while he took up a covering position. "Can you start either motor?"

"Sure."

Another three-round burst of gunfire chipped away at the knot of mangroves they'd used as a dock the other night.

Behind him Addi cried out and his blood turned to ice. "Are you hit?"

"No."

"Andy?"

"No." Her voice was choked with tears.

He turned. Addi had gathered Andy into a tight embrace, blocking the boy's view of the boats. "Oh, no." He saw the body of an older man with graying hair and a rangy build floating facedown in the water behind one of the boats. Produce, dry goods and a box of sodas were scattered around the body.

"It's Nico." She gulped, struggling for composure.

"Addi, I'm sorry."

"Nico?" Andy asked, straining for a look.

"You keep your eyes on the water," Drew instructed him. At seven—nearly eight—he didn't need to stare death in the face. "Let me know if you see anything moving out there."

"Okay."

He wanted to comfort them both, but escaping was the priority.

"Can you get the other boat in the water?"

She nodded as another shot splintered the stilt. Drew fired into the trees, hoping to pin back Everett's men for just another minute or so.

"Ready."

He heard the motor start. "Go on, then. Leave the bag."

"Not without you."

"I'll catch up." The boat wasn't that fast. "Stay near the bank."

He heard a splash, then the rumble as the motor revved.

Spotting movement at the tree line, he squeezed off a three-shot burst and the pained scream confirmed he'd hit flesh. He could hold off Everett's men, giving Addi and Andy time to get away. Someone on this swamp would help her. He just had to give them the chance. He'd been trained to hold the line and—

"Drew!"

It was Andy's screech that tugged him away from that sucking abyss that whispered he was only good enough as a sacrificial distraction. They'd warned him about moments like these when the past would cloud the present. Although he was more than willing to do whatever kept Addi and the boy safe, this wasn't the best place to make a stand.

How could he have forgotten about the other team on an attack boat? She needed him. Too much swamp remained between her and Casey's protection. Drew reached into the bag and pulled out both transmitters. He shoved one into his pocket and toggled the switch on the other, tucking it into the mud near the mangroves. Assuming it didn't get shot to pieces or carried away by an animal, it would give Casey's men a place to start searching and hopefully result in a decent burial for Nico.

As Addi urged the boat out into deeper water, Drew scrambled along the bank, trading fire with the men behind them. Anticipating the best place to join her, he hollered and pointed. She waved back, acknowledging. There was something to be said for knowing a person well.

"Mom, wait for him!" Andy's cry carried across the air, filling him with determination. He wouldn't miss, wouldn't renege on his promise to see her and Andy through this.

When Drew glanced their way, the boy was lying low in the boat, his head barely visible.

Whatever Addi had said had calmed him down. They had a great kid, he thought, rounding the point and jumping into the water. He ignored the idea of any wildlife as he trudged through the waist-deep water to the waiting boat. He came up to the side, tossed in the drenched gear and wet gun first, then pulled himself in.

His boots were barely clear of the water before Addi gunned the motor. The bow reared up a little before the boat leveled to skim across the swamp.

Heedless of his soaked clothing, Andy crawled closer to give him a hug. "Seventy-three seconds."

Ah, so she'd distracted him by making him timekeeper again. "Is that good?"

Andy shook his head. "It was too long without you."

"But I made it." He gave his son's shoulder a squeeze.

Andy nodded. "I'm glad a gator didn't get you."

"I'm glad the bad guys didn't get you."

Another hug. Drew thought he could get used to this.

"Are you going to stay with us forever?"

He looked back at Addi, but she didn't seem to hear anything over the growl of the motor and her eyes were on the water ahead of them. "That's up to your mom." But he sure hoped it worked out that way.

"But she's gonna have a baby. You have to

stay and be the dad for it." His face clouded with worry, that familiar Bryant frown creasing his brow.

"What?"

"You and her were kissing. I saw. Kissing makes babies."

Drew was not getting into *this* right now. "Andy, the three of us have a lot to talk about."

"I want you to be my dad."

"I'd be honored." It was the best he could do, considering the poor timing of this conversation. "The three of us will— Get down!" he shouted as another attack boat approached behind them. He pushed Andy to the little protection offered by the hull of their shallow flat-bottomed boat and reached for the shotgun. It was the only dry weapon.

Addi twisted around, then swerved across the swamp as she searched for cover behind an outcropping of trees. Their boat wasn't fast or agile and Everett's men had no intention of allowing them out of this swamp.

A warning shot fired from the shore just as she made the turn. Though Drew was prepared to shoot back, it wasn't worth the risk of Andy getting hit in the cross fire.

They'd been flanked by a team of professionals. The best they could do was surrender and hope the orders were to take them in alive. "Time to cooperate," he said, lowering the shotgun and raising his hands.

Her face went pale, but she nodded, cutting the motor and raising her hands, as well.

A voice boomed from shore, "Addison Collins!"

She faced the man shouting at her. "Yes?"

"Mr. Everett wants you to come with us. Put up a fight and we'll shoot you where you are."

"I promise you I'll find a better opportunity," Drew said under his breath. Or he'd die trying.

"*We* will find a better opportunity," she said, her mouth set in a grim line.

The attack boat came up alongside them, the leader clearly irritated by their resistance. "I'll come with you," Addi replied when they demanded it. "Just let my son go."

Drew was impressed by her courage, knew she had to ask, but he wanted to keep Andy with them.

"All of you or none of you," the leader said, raising an assault rifle.

"Be reasonable. He's a child."

"Would you rather I let him go right here in the swamp?"

Based on what Drew had seen, it wouldn't be much of a hardship for Andy, but he kept that opinion to himself.

"Well?" the leader demanded.

"All of us." Addi sent Drew an apologetic look as the men tossed them a line and tied their small boat to the attack boat.

He knew she'd weighed the decision and he murmured reassurances as he kept Andy tucked by his side. None of them, not even Andy, said a word as they were towed through the swamp to a dock and transferred to a big black SUV waiting there.

Chapter Fifteen

Drew reviewed the limited options as the SUV barreled down the road in the direction of New Orleans. The driver, weaving in and out of traffic, clearly wasn't worried about the authorities intervening.

Drew had the second transmitter in his pocket, but his hands were cuffed. The crew was well armed. Drew recognized the semiautomatic pistols in each holster and assumed the men were more than proficient. So far the five-man team had shown a disturbing level of efficiency and a cold calm that only cranked up Drew's adrenaline response. He was now certain that last night's seeming inept work by these guys had been about ensuring that Addi was captured alive.

He reminded himself that he'd survived hell once already. Nothing Everett dreamed up could be worse than what Drew had endured as a POW. Yes, there was more on the line beyond his own life, but he would not cave to the fear of failure.

He didn't know Craig Everett beyond the little insight Addi had shared, but the man had been given an excellent strike team. Casey would be very interested in this development.

The city came into view and Drew waited for his opening, knowing it would be a narrow window. With a clear path to a weapon, he could flip the whole scenario to their favor. Every fiber of his being was braced to save Addi and Andy from whatever Everett had planned.

He and Addi had been cuffed at the wrist with plastic zip ties, but Andy's hands were free and the boy was buckled into the seat between them. Drew wasn't naive enough to believe that minor concession was a positive thing. Everett was working for someone connected and ruthless.

The driver slowed down as the traffic got heavier. Drew leaned over Andy's head. "Whatever happens," he murmured to Addison, "whatever they do, don't tell them anything."

Her eyes welled with unshed tears, but she gave him a smidgen of a nod.

"We'll get through this. All three of us." He bumped his elbow against Andy's shoulder in a small show of assurance as the driver turned down a narrow alley between two warehouses.

Drew believed Casey and his team of Specialists had to be closing in. Thinking anything else would erode his confidence. He ran through a mental checklist of the details Addi's former fiancé didn't know about her. His men might've found them in the bayou, but not because of Everett's knowledge of her past.

Had to be that leaky contact. Had to be, Drew thought again. Everett wouldn't have wasted time searching for Addi around her college haunts if she'd told him her real origins or given him any indication how much she valued her family roots.

The car slammed into Park and the driver cut the engine. Drew decided not to dwell on the obvious concern that their captors weren't hiding location or faces. He'd cheated death plenty and intended to keep up his winning record now that he had two amazing reasons to stay alive. The men in the front seat climbed out and the back doors opened a moment later, flooding the vehicle with bright morning light.

Drew hopped down, hiding his trepidation behind a cocky squint. "Nice place."

"Shut up," the driver said, pushing him toward the nearest door.

New Orleans was a fine town, but this grimy industrial area wasn't the sort of area preferred by a man like Everett. This seedy environment was, however, just the sort of place Drew could navigate with expertise. Places like this lurked in the shadowy corners all over the globe, always controlled by the man with the most money and biggest weapons.

Gang graffiti decorated nearly every rusting surface. Drew wondered how much Everett's men had paid, in dollars or blood, to gain temporary control of this area. The ripe scents of trash, grease and stale fuel stained the thick, humid air. Drew hoped to turn his unfortunate affinity and experience with this kind of place into an advantage. Surely the powers that be would grant him that much, giving him a chance to create something good from the sorry remnants of his career.

"Where are we?"

Andy's small voice sliced right into Drew's heart.

"I'm not sure," Addi said, "but we're together."

Drew didn't turn, picturing mother and son holding hands as Everett's men pushed them into the dreary interior of the warehouse. Two cars were parked near a wide garage door. Three battered couches and an oversize flat-screen television made up a seating area in the far corner. The windows of what might have been a supervisor's office were covered with peeling black paint. An odd mix of industrial equipment was scattered around the space, but the stack of crates along one wall looked too new to be anything but valuable.

Drugs or guns. Drew hoped like hell this gang was the gunrunning sort. He could hardly beat the crap out of this crew with drugs. He needed a weapon.

The office door opened as they approached and out stepped Everett, looking preppy in a short-sleeved polo shirt, creased khaki slacks and loafers; Drew understood Addi's comment about polish and charm. It wasn't hard to picture them as an attractive power couple, able to give Andy every advantage. Drew wanted to bloody that smug face beyond all recognition.

"Addison, so good to see you again." Ignoring Drew, Everett reached for her hands, hesitating when he saw she was cuffed. "That's ridiculous. Take those off."

The driver shook his head. "Not recommended."

Drew smothered a grin, remembering how Addi had clocked the other man when he'd grabbed Andy with too much force.

"She won't hurt me," Everett insisted. To Addi, he said, "This can be over in minutes. A few answers and you and Andy can be on your way."

The driver made a snorting sound as he sliced through the zip ties binding Addi's hands. Whatever delusions Everett was under, Drew knew they weren't supposed to survive this meeting.

As soon as her hands were free, Addi slapped Everett across the face hard enough to knock him back a step. The red handprint bloomed instantly across his freshly shaved cheek. Drew wanted to crow with pride.

"Told you so," the driver muttered.

"Screw you," Everett said to the driver. "Keep these two under control." He shoved Addi toward the office. "I just need a few minutes."

Drew knew she wouldn't break, yet it took all his willpower not to make eye contact as Everett led her away. Neither Everett nor his men could know how invested he was, or they'd kill him where he stood.

ADDISON HEARD CRAIG close the door behind her and she rubbed her elbow where his hand had dug hard into her arm. In all the time she'd known him, he'd never shown a ruthless side. Oh, she'd known he was a formidable force in a financial negotiation or conference room, she'd known he kept fit, but he'd never demonstrated this dark edge. She supposed that was why the truth of his illegal dealings had been such a shock.

He shoved her into a cold metal folding chair and leaned back against an old metal desk, folding his arms across his chest. "Let's do this the easy way," he suggested. "Tell me what you think you know and who you've told about your theories."

"What theories?"

"This isn't a game or a courtroom, Addison.

You ran away from home flinging accusations at me." His quiet, unflappable tone strained her composure. "It's been expensive tracking you down and I intend to make sure the investment was worth it." He reached out, running a fingertip across her sunburned cheek. "You forgot the sunblock."

She refused to flinch. If he was focused on her, Drew could get Andy out of harm's way. Getting that sunburn while her men had been fishing might be the last truly happy moment of her life. She wouldn't let Craig cheapen it. "How did you find me?"

He shook his head, his eyes hard as stone. "I'll ask the questions. You'll answer them."

"And then you'll let us go," she said, refusing to make it a question. Though he nodded she wasn't buying it. She wanted to rail, to shout and scream that he wouldn't get away with any of this. Not after what he'd done and what she assumed he would do in the coming moments.

"Addison, who have you talked to?"

"No one." Technically it was true. Talking to Drew didn't count, as he was officially "deceased" and she hadn't shared any details of Craig's activities. She'd sent emails and one snail mail package as insurance. Her stomach clenched as she realized that insurance would be used if Craig had his way here.

He blew out a heavy sigh. "You're wasting my time. I wouldn't have been arrested unless you blew the whistle on me. You're the only one who had access."

She pulled on the composure that had served her so well through depositions and negotiations during her legal career. "I don't have any idea what you mean."

Craig leaned forward, his lips twisted in a menacing grin. "Why did you run from home?"

She nearly blurted out the "adventure" answer she'd given to Andy, but she didn't want to divert Craig's attention. "There was a death in the family. My presence was requested."

"Bull." Craig leaned back. "You don't have any family beyond your son."

"That isn't true." Mama Leonie was family. Nico was family. Bernadette and Professor Hastings were family. Maybe not by blood, but some bonds went deeper, some roots were stronger. She didn't expect a money-grubbing sellout like Craig to understand that.

"Answer me!" Craig shouted. "Who else have you told?"

She shook her head. "No one."

Craig grabbed her shoulders, shaking her hard enough to make her teeth clack together. "Addison, cooperate." The chair rocked back when he released her with a violent shove. "Answer my questions now or I can't protect you."

A chill of fear skittered down her spine. She didn't fight it, embracing it instead and using it to hold her ground. "I have nothing to say to you, Craig."

He stared at her for another long moment, then moved around her chair and tapped twice on the door. In the interminable silence, she heard the squeak and scrape of footsteps in the warehouse coming closer to the office.

Two men hauled in Drew and tied him to a chair at the other end of the room. Addison felt a wave of dread. Her hope of him saving Andy fizzled and died. Her son was alone with these terrible men. She had to find a way out of this nightmare or her dream of a family would be crushed again.

"Who is this?" Craig demanded.

My heart. My love. "A friend," she said, hoping to protect Drew.

Craig snorted. "Here's how it will go, Addison," he began. "I'll ask you a question. You'll answer me, or your *friend* will suffer. Is that clear?"

"We don't know anything about your problems," she replied. Drew didn't want her to talk, so she wouldn't talk.

"We'll find out, won't we?"

She kept her gaze on Craig, not risking eye

contact with Drew. If Craig discovered this was Andy's real father, if he discovered how much she loved him, Drew would pay. And he'd already been through more than any person should endure.

"Why did you run from San Francisco?"

"I came out here to help a family in need," she replied honestly. She and Andy were a family, and they'd definitely needed to get away from Craig.

Craig raised a finger and one of the men behind Drew came around and punched him in the belly.

She closed her eyes. "That was an honest answer."

Craig bent over, bracing his hands on his knees to look her in the eye. "They are going to rig a battery to your friend and electrocute him for every lie you tell me."

"Craig, this is insane. I can't help you."

He gave another signal and suddenly Drew's body jerked and seized. Addison's resolve faltered.

"Don't talk, Addi," Drew rasped as his body recovered.

"Addi?" Craig turned on his heel. "You told me you despised that nickname, that it was weak."

"Is there a question in there?"

Craig flung an arm toward Drew. "Who is he to you?"

"My best friend," she said as her heart raced

on with more of the truth she would never share with Craig. *My heart. My should-be husband. My son's father. My soul mate.* She'd been delusional to believe she could be satisfied with bland contentment when she harbored all this passion for Drew. Alive or dead, no one else had meant the same to her. Or to Andy.

"I was your best friend. We were supposed to be on our honeymoon now."

"With blood money!" she shouted, furious.

"It all spends the same," Craig said with a slimy smirk. "You can't judge me, Addison. I know who your clients are and how you 'negotiate.'" He mocked her with air quotes.

"I never traded innocent lives for personal gain!"

"No?" Craig signaled and Drew's body started quaking again.

"Stop it!"

"Tell me who you've told."

"Don't talk!" Drew whispered between electricity-induced spasms.

Addison wouldn't dishonor Drew by giving in now, no matter how much it hurt her to watch him suffer. "We'll get out of this," she promised.

"You want out of this? Tell me the truth!"

Addison shook her head.

Craig scrubbed a hand over his mouth and closed his eyes. "Get the boy."

"No!" Drew and Addison shouted at the same time, but Craig's men were already moving, dragging Drew away.

Tears streaked down her face. "You can't do this," she cried out. "He trusts you."

"Your choice," Craig said as Andy was led into the office. "Whatever happens now is on you."

Andy's eyes were wide as they led him to another chair out of her reach. "Mama?"

She blinked away the tears, determined to be strong for her son. "Don't worry. We'll be out of here soon." As long as Drew was breathing, as long as her heart beat, they would see that Andy survived.

"Well?" Craig raised a finger, bringing those horrific battery cables too close to her son's small body.

The blood in her veins turned to ice. "If you so much as pluck a hair from his head, I'll kill you."

Craig laughed. "Start talking, Addison, or I'll prove just what an incompetent and incapable mother you are."

She swallowed, her jaw clenched as she tried to smile at her son. "Andy, get your stopwatch ready." Anything to distract him. "Press Start when I say go and Stop when I stop talking."

"'Kay." He chewed on his lower lip as he concentrated.

"Go." She met Craig's hard gaze. "About six

weeks ago, while I was cooking dinner, your phone beeped with a text message and I checked it. One of the names was familiar. You remember the ambassador's assistant arrested for human trafficking?"

Craig scowled, gesturing for her to continue.

"Curious and a bit worried on your behalf, I started doing some digging into your financials. I didn't actually speak to anyone about you. I gave the authorities a place to start looking into a troubling association. I trusted that if you were innocent you'd cooperate. If you had been innocent they wouldn't have arrested you."

"But you left town."

Andy interrupted, announcing the time on his watch. She beamed at him. "Good job."

She looked up at Craig. "I left because I didn't want Andy getting dragged into your problems."

"Too late."

"Apparently," she agreed. "How did you find us?"

"It doesn't matter."

Oh, she was sure that it did. If Craig's contacts had compromised Drew's friend Casey, they were out of allies.

"Who else did you notify about your discovery?"

She shook her head.

"How many volts do you think his little body can take?"

"Shut up, Craig," she snapped, adrenaline pounding through her system. She might not have Drew's skills, but she had the benefit of being in full-blown mama-bear mode. "I've cooperated. Now let us go. I promise you'll never hear from us again."

"Not so fast. I know you too well. You always have a contingency plan."

"Not this time," she insisted. "There wasn't any time. Discovering what you've been doing spooked me. I did what I could, then did what I felt best protected Andy."

"I don't believe you."

She shrugged. "That isn't my problem. You did this to yourself," she started, unable to keep a leash on her temper. "Quit lashing out at us with your guilty conscience. I've answered your questions. Now let us go."

"Who else knows, Addison?"

"No one!" Professor Hastings wouldn't open the package unless she failed to make contact on the tenth.

"I'm satisfied," a voice declared. Addison hadn't noticed the cell phone on the desktop. Craig must have had it on speaker this entire time. "Clean up and come in."

"Yes, sir," Craig said, his face a mixture of

relief and regret. He tucked the phone into his pocket and turned to the men flanking Andy. "You heard him. Let's clean up."

Addison cringed as they urged her son out of the chair. He raced across the room and took her hand. "It'll be okay," she said, determined those words wouldn't become a lie. "You did a great job."

"I know," he said, his smile wobbling. "Drew told me the secret of how to be brave."

"Good." Probably some quote from one of their favorite comic books. Whatever it was, she was grateful for the positive influence. Andy's hand felt so small in her grasp. She vowed to find a way out of this. Her son would grow into a man and she and Drew would be there to watch and support him along the way. She had to seize the first opportunity, she thought, praying she'd recognize it. "You'll have to tell me that secret sometime," she said as they were shoved roughly into the back of one of the cars parked inside the warehouse.

"But he said you taught the secret to him."

"Is that so?"

"Did you forget it?"

"Of course not," she said, though she had no idea what secret Drew had credited to her. Whatever it was made Andy feel better and that was the important factor.

"I love you," Andy said, scooting across the backseat of the car to sit close to her side. "Where are we going now?"

"I'm not sure," she admitted, battling back fear. *Where had they taken Drew?*

The driver twisted around to face them. "You like to swim, kid?"

"Yes," Andy replied warily.

"Well, I'm supposed to find the perfect swamp swimming hole for you," he said with a nasty smile.

Addison didn't need a translator to get the hidden meaning. Craig—or whoever was calling the shots here—planned to silence them permanently. "I don't have my swimsuit, Mom."

"It'll be okay," she assured him.

"Or dry clothes. Or a place to put my watch," he added. A worried frown clouded his face.

She wanted to tear Craig apart for this. "We'll figure it out," she said. "I don't want you to worry about anything."

"We can't leave without Drew!"

She glanced around, seeing no sign of him. "He'll find us," she said. Or they would find him. She wasn't giving him up without a fight, whether or not he wanted to stay in their lives after this.

"Oh, you'll see him soon, kid. It'll be a regular family picnic."

With that cryptic comment the driver started

the car. The big overhead bay door rose with a groan and scrape of neglected metal and a rattle of chains across a squeaky pulley.

As bright sunlight flooded the space, Addison shielded her eyes against the glare. This man planned to kill her and her son out in the swamp, where nature would be more than happy to clean up the mess. Odd as it sounded, even in her thoughts, she felt a surge of gratitude that Craig knew so little about her.

Chapter Sixteen

From the backseat of the black SUV, Drew watched the white sedan pull out of the warehouse and take the lead. He had three men with him, two in the front seats and one back here with him. That left only one or two with Addi and Andy, which gave her a fighting chance.

He'd heard the orders to dump their bodies in the swamp and had been overwhelmed with relief when he'd seen her and their son walking to the car rather than being carried. No big surprise that Everett was too squeamish to do the dirty work.

When Everett had taken Addi into the office, Drew had used the distraction to turn on the transmitter. With Andy's help, he'd managed to drop the device into the couch where they'd been ordered to wait. He hoped Casey could mobilize a team quickly enough to snare Everett.

Now if only his body would just get over the inconvenient and unexpected electric shock. It felt as though his blood would never stop sizzling.

His thoughts were clear, which was a plus, and any pain was repressed by his determination to rescue his wife and son.

Wife. The word was as soothing, as easy in his mind as swinging gently in a hammock on a shady porch. He wasn't sure when his brain had finally accepted the status his heart had never relinquished. He wasn't sure it mattered. Whether he had to wait an hour or another ten years for her to love him again, Addi was his wife in every way that mattered. No one would tear them apart again and no one would cheat him of another precious minute as a family.

"Can I have some water?" He tipped his head toward the bottle of water in the cup holder in the console.

"No," said the man seated next to him.

Drew snorted. "Are you planning to give me a last meal?"

"Hell no." This denial came from the driver. "You don't have long to suffer."

Through the windshield, Drew saw the sedan with Addi and Andy two car lengths ahead. No other guards were in her car and both drivers were being very cautious on the return trip to the bayou.

"A little compassion could make a big difference," Drew said.

"Compassion? For who?" The guard in the

passenger seat snorted. "I'll shoot you right here if you don't shut your trap."

"You shut up," the driver balked. "Unless you want to detail his brains out of the upholstery."

"Why work that hard? We can dump the car near the projects and it's someone else's problem."

Drew nearly laughed as the men argued with each other, confident their captive was no threat. Keep believing that, he thought, fueling the delusion by slumping in his seat and leaning against the door.

They left the paved roads a few minutes later, following the sedan into the shady wilds of the bayou. This part of the world had always intrigued him with how quickly the terrain shifted from polished civilization to raw and unforgiving. Of course, the dangers shifted, too, from man to nature. At least nature didn't pick sides; it went after any threatening intrusion with equal fervor.

"Better head deeper," Drew muttered. "You dump us here and our bodies will pop up too soon."

"What do you know about it?"

"More than you do if you're thinking of stopping here."

"Ignore him," the guard in the front passenger seat said. "We do it the way the boss wants."

"Does your boss even understand the bayous?"

The guard in the backseat plowed a big fist into Drew's jaw. "You're wasting your last words."

Drew shrugged but kept silent. Wherever they stopped, he knew which man in this car to attack first. He only hoped Addi had figured out the same weak link in her car.

He hated that she and Andy were scared, but he also knew she had a well of strength and courage to draw from. Any woman who'd raised a child dealt with any number of false alarms and real scares on her own. Andy was a good kid, but that didn't mean he hadn't stirred up his fair share of trouble along the way. Addi's courage wouldn't falter, despite the overwhelming odds. The soul-deep fighter in her hadn't changed.

When he lined that up with her insider knowledge of the swamps and bayous out here, he felt a ray of hope flickering like sunlight through the cypress branches high above. Everett might have hired quality muscle to do his dirty work, but Drew and Addi held the real advantage.

Smart men would take them way back into the bayou, shoot them and sink their bodies in the deepest water. He didn't think this crew would be that patient. A few minutes later the team proved him right as they followed a dusty service track into a protected wildlife area.

"Triple homicide on federal land." He shook his head. "That won't end well for you."

The guard in the backseat pulled his gun and aimed it at Drew's temple. "You were saying?"

Drew stared him down, willing his body to hold still. The best time to strike was yet to come. He let them pull him from the car and managed to maintain an outward air of defeat as the driver of the sedan hauled Addi and Andy to the bank of the swamp.

It was as if time slowed, each second standing well apart from the previous and the next. Every beat of his heart might have been as long as a minute as his mind cataloged each detail. His senses were primed, his body ready to react. Drew felt the brush of the air on his skin, heard the rustling of leaves above and the absolute silence of the mirrorlike water.

Only one other time had he felt this timeless, out-of-body sensation. He looked around as they prodded him to stand next to his son. No surprise how Everett's men planned to proceed. The guard with the gun would raise his arm and it would be a simple double-tap to the back of each skull. In moments, the only two people he loved in this world would be dead before their bodies fell into the water, a feast for the scavengers.

Andy, his hands free, reached up to hold Drew's cuffed hands. "Mom says it'll be okay."

Drew looked down into those wide brown eyes, so like his, and saw more awareness than any nearly eight-year-old kid should know. "She's right." One way or another they would all be okay. He scanned the water and what he could see of the banks. Whatever the next moments held, he would ensure the two of them made it out alive.

Over their son's head he met Addi's gaze. Her eyes were bright, lit with the dangerous fire of a protective mother ready to do battle. "Trust me?" He slid his gaze to the water and back to her.

She smiled at him. "Always."

Behind them the men were debating who should shoot Andy. Drew shifted his weight, bracing his feet wide. His hands gripping Andy's, he twisted around. "Let the kid go."

"Hell no," the man who'd driven the sedan said.

"He's a kid." Drew was trying to push anything that might resemble a sympathy button in one of these four bastards. "A little kid."

"Who shouldn't spend the rest of his life missing his mommy." The sedan driver circled his finger. "We're doing him a favor," he sneered. "Now cooperate and we'll make it quick. For them," he added with a laugh.

Drew shook his head. "I'm sorry, son." He squeezed Andy's wrists. Turning back to the water, he tossed Andy out into the shallow water of the swamp.

Reacting instantly, Addi lunged for the nearest

of Everett's men, taking him down with a shoulder tackle a professional football player would envy.

It amazed Drew that he could fall any deeper in love with the woman, especially amid a fight for their lives, but it happened.

Guns fired in a rapid burst of violent noise, but Drew didn't care. Andy would find shelter, Addi was holding her own with one guard and the three remaining men were no real challenge. He rushed forward to safeguard his family, feeling a smile bloom across his face as he swung his restrained hands out, batting away the executioner's gun, then plowing an elbow into the man's jaw. When he dropped to all fours, Drew kicked him hard enough to crack ribs and leave him breathless. "Stay down," he growled, picking up the man's gun.

A blow to Drew's kidneys caused more irritation than pain and he countered with a sharp, swinging kick to the second man's head. He put a bullet through his knee to keep him down and tucked that pistol into his waistband. Three down, one to go.

"Andy?" he called out.

"He's safe," Addi replied.

Drew glanced back and saw Addi holding the guard she'd tackled at gunpoint. "Shoot the tires,"

Drew shouted as the weak link from the SUV raced for the vehicles.

She put a bullet into one tire on each car, even as the jerk turned and shot recklessly in their direction. Drew's vision turned red at the edges and he fired back, calling out to confirm Addi hadn't been hit.

The man dropped his gun and begged for mercy, scooting backward as Drew advanced. "I'll cooperate, give a statement, whatever you want," he stammered.

"How thoughtful." Drew backhanded him. "You missed your chance for any mercy from me."

"Drew," Addi said from behind him. "We're okay."

"We'll put them in the sedan and push it into the swamp," he said.

"You can't do that," the man with cracked ribs protested. "Th-the gators!"

Drew stood tall, keeping the gun on the pleading man. "You're right. We could get fined for animal abuse."

"I'm willing to risk it if you are," Addi said, coming up beside him.

He just stared at her, amazed and grateful. "Where's Andy?"

"Safe," she assured him. "He scrambled up the bank and into a tree."

Drew followed her gaze. Andy's clothes were wet, but he was tucked in tight in the strong bracket of a tree. "Good job."

"My watch still works!" He pumped his small fist. "Can I come down and help push the car?"

Drew thought it sounded like a fine idea. "Sure."

He stepped back, swaying a bit. His vision blurred, making it difficult to get his bearings. "Addi?"

"Right here."

He didn't believe her; her voice sounded too far away. The adrenaline had carried him this far, but on the downward slope of the rush, he felt the wounds where a bullet, maybe two, had tagged him. "No big deal, Addi. Take Andy... get safe..." He couldn't catch his breath, felt his heart thundering in his chest. He shook his head to clear his vision, but it didn't help.

"I'm not leaving you. Let me take a look."

Stupid to shoot out the car tires, he thought, sliding hard to the ground as his knees gave. He should've had her shoot the bastard. He tried to slow his thoughts, reassess his injuries. Damn it, this wasn't about blood loss or injury. They were only flesh wounds. He was having a panic attack.

"I'll be fine," he said through clenched teeth. He shook his wrists. "Get these off of me."

He told himself he'd done well and had held it

together when it mattered. Still, they weren't off the hook yet. Everett's men were down for now, but the survival instinct would have them attacking Addi again if they had an opportunity.

Drew tried to stand, but Addi held him down with a firm hand on his shoulder. "Stay put a minute."

He stared up at the sky, hoping the clear blue day would calm him down. No such luck. He closed his eyes tight, fighting against the useless anxiety. She still needed him. He needed his body to get back on task. He heard her snapping out orders and felt his hands finally drop free. A small weight landed on his chest and he opened his eyes as Andy wrapped his skinny arms around Drew in a fierce hug.

"What's wrong with you?" Andy asked.

What wasn't wrong with him? How could he explain post-traumatic stress and a full-blown panic attack in terms Andy would understand? "I'll be okay in a minute."

"You got shot."

Drew glanced at his biceps where blood stained the torn sleeve of his gray T-shirt. "Looks like it."

"Does it hurt?"

"Not much." Not nearly as much as fighting the fear that he'd be locked up again, away from his son and the woman who should be his wife.

"Then why don't you breathe right?"

"Andy, hush," Addi scolded.

"He's fine," Drew said on a weak laugh, waving off her concern. His breath shuddered in and out and his lungs resumed normal function. To his surprise, answering the questions helped give him a focal point, something the shrinks suggested early in his treatment when the memories and nightmares had overwhelmed him.

"Did you see which one of them shot me?"

"That one." Andy pointed to one of the men on the ground near the edge of the swamp. "You kick really high."

"Thanks." He ruffled his son's hair. "The army taught me."

"Like Captain America?"

"I think the shield would've been helpful."

"You could've knocked them all out with one throw. Before…"

Drew saw the moment Andy remembered Nico. He pulled Andy in for a hard hug. "The bad guys will pay for everything they did. Your mom and I will see to that."

"If Nico could've kicked like you…"

It wouldn't have made any difference, but Drew understood the real problem. "Want me to teach you that kick?"

Andy nodded. "Will you throw me again? It was fun."

"Maybe later." Into the clear water of a pool.

Between guns and alligators, he'd known this particular corner of the bayou was the lesser danger.

Andy looked from Drew to his mom. "What'll we do with all of 'em now?"

"I'm still for putting them in the swamp," Drew said.

"Me, too," Andy crowed, bouncing to his feet. "Let's go."

"Drew," Addi chided. "What happened to caring about the wildlife?"

"If we use the sedan, someone will come haul it out sooner rather than later. It's a classic."

She rolled her eyes. "Fine."

The man protested as he and the others were loaded at gunpoint into the car. None of them seemed to realize what Addi had known from the start: the swamp wasn't terribly deep here. The men would be uncomfortable and, because of their ignorance, they'd be too frightened to move. Hopefully that fear would give law enforcement time to get out here and arrest the four of them.

ADDISON WATCHED, TRYING not to laugh, when the bargaining started. The four men had no idea they were safer in the swamp than on dry land with her. She was more than a little disconcerted knowing how easy it would've been, how good it would've felt to kill the men so willing to murder her family.

Family. It was a beautiful word and it felt more real now than it had since her ruined wedding day.

She kept sneaking looks at Drew as he and Andy pushed the car into the water. If anything nibbled at those four men in the car, she wouldn't be the least bit sorry for it. She'd had her chance, known as she held the gun that a self-defense plea would've assured her acquittal, but she'd managed to do the right thing. In no small part because her son was watching, but she'd taken her cues from Drew, as well.

She'd been awestruck watching him fight, heedless of the personal danger as he overpowered the other armed guards. Her mind zipped back to the moment before the fight, when nothing more than a look had fully explained his intentions.

How was it they still had that connection? Without words, she'd known he would get Andy out of harm's way. She hadn't expected him to throw Andy into the swamp, but knowing the threat in the water was minimal so close to the service road, it made perfect sense.

The men shouted, screamed, really, as the car partially filled with water. She had zero sympathy, smiling as Drew and Andy swaggered back to join her near the SUV. "There's a spare tire."

Drew grinned and her pulse fluttered. "That will get us back to town."

"Then what?"

"I suggest we find a landline and make a phone call so Everett doesn't slip away."

"I'd like to wring his neck."

"Because he fooled you?" Andy asked.

How much had Andy heard the other night? Or today, for that matter?

"That's one reason." Addi wondered how best to answer the question. Only a few weeks ago he'd looked up to Craig as a father figure. "He did some bad things," she began carefully, searching for the right words. "When we met him, when we let him be part of our lives, I think he was more of a good guy."

"He changed?"

"Yes." Drew knelt down, looking Andy right in the eye. "Craig Everett was good to you once, right?"

"Yes." Andy's eyes gleamed with tears. "I don't want him to marry us anymore."

"Not a chance," Addison said, smoothing his hair back from his face. "You never have to see him again."

"He won't ever be my dad?"

"Absolutely not," Addison replied, looking at

Drew. They really needed to tell their son the truth. But it felt like a big risk when she didn't know what kind of life Drew wanted.

Bodyguard duty was one thing. Rekindling their friendship and rediscovering their long-buried passion was understandable. But what did Drew want from her after this crisis was over?

He'd made the choice once before—to leave her alone with her new life. She understood his reasoning but couldn't help wondering what choice he'd make now.

"Let's get that tire changed and get moving," Drew said, interrupting her thoughts. "I don't want to risk them getting brave enough to bolt."

"They can't be brave," Andy said as she boosted him into the backseat.

"What do you mean?" she asked.

"The secret to bravery," he replied, clearly exasperated to be stating the obvious.

Except it wasn't obvious to her.

"They don't have someone to love," Andy said. "Or someone who loves them back to make them brave. Did I get it right, Drew?"

"You sure did."

Addison stared at Drew for a moment before realizing that he needed her help changing the flat tire. He called out for Andy to time them. They finished in record time. She rounded the car and climbed into the driver's seat.

"Maybe I should stay," he muttered, his gaze on the partially submerged sedan as if he were suddenly uncertain where they went from here. "I can make sure they don't get away."

"No." She wasn't letting him out of her sight. Not until they had things well and truly settled. "We stick together."

Chapter Seventeen

The drive back into the city went by in a blur and Addison's thoughts were a jumble of questions she couldn't answer. Questions for Drew, but she wouldn't ask until she had a few answers for herself. What did she want next? Returning to San Francisco felt wrong, even if she took the rest of the summer to help Nico's family recover from the devastating loss.

What if she moved back home? Was this a better place to raise her son?

"Don't worry, Addi," Drew said. "Everett won't escape."

"It's not that."

"No?" He sounded surprised "Then what?"

"Just about everything else," she admitted. "But it can wait until we know Craig is in custody and we get you patched up."

Drew nodded, his lips pressed into a thin line.

"Are you hurting?"

He shook his head. "Let's drive by the warehouse."

"Okay." She knew he wouldn't put them in danger, and this time they had the advantage of loaded guns. "I still think we should've used one of the phones."

"We can't risk tipping off Everett's contact and giving whoever the hell it is another head start."

"It's hard to fathom any one person having this kind of reach."

"You took extreme measures when you fled."

"I did." And Drew had found her anyway. She glanced into the backseat, pleased to see Andy gazing out the window. Bless his heart. She didn't want all this to haunt his dreams. He was just a little boy.

Sirens blared in the oncoming lanes, and law enforcement vehicles sped their way before veering toward the warehouse Craig had been hiding in.

"I hope they're on our side," she said, goose bumps raising the hair on her arms. If Craig managed to escape again, she might never be free.

"Let's stop here," Drew said.

Addison pulled to a halt behind the perimeter created by men in various law enforcement uniforms.

"Open your door slowly," he instructed Addison. "Andy, stay right where you are."

"Yes, sir," her little brave boy affirmed.

"Oh!" She pointed through the windshield. "There's Craig." Her breath caught in her chest. "In handcuffs." She hoped it wasn't just for show.

"Consider him locked down for good," Drew said. A satisfied smile tilted his lips.

"How can you be sure?"

"Because the man next to him is Thomas Casey. The guy who recruited me to find you."

She wanted to believe, to share Drew's confidence. "You sound sure of him."

"There's only one other person I trust as much." His eyes darted to the rearview mirror. "Well, two."

Addison looked at him, but Andy asked the question she couldn't find her voice to pose. "You mean you trust him like you trust us?"

He nodded, holding Addison's gaze. "I do."

This wasn't the time for tears, but she'd pined all of Andy's young life to hear those two words from Drew.

He reached across the seat and brushed away the tear that rolled down her cheek. "Don't worry," he said softly, somehow understanding her fears. "We'll figure everything out."

She nodded, her throat clogged with her heart and all her churning emotions. Hope and love were easy to identify, but they were shadowed by uncertainty. She knew what she wanted, but would Drew want that, too?

The man Drew pointed out turned their way, striding through the chaos to meet them. "Come on," Drew said. "I'll introduce you and then you'll understand why I'm so confident this is the last you'll see of Everett."

"All right," she managed, wanting to believe him. As Drew made introductions, Addison studied Director Casey. There was a hard edge under the business-casual polish, but his sincerity as he addressed her son won her over.

"Do you have enough information now?" she asked abruptly, unable to tolerate any more small talk.

"I might have a few more questions, but thanks to both of you, the trap my deputy set worked perfectly. We have Everett as well as his contact inside the Department of State."

Addison sucked in a breath and looked at Drew, thinking of the implications. "That is a long reach." Department of State personnel were typically informed of military operations around the globe. An insider leak like that might even have led to Drew's capture.

"Well, it's cut short now. I anticipate closure on several questionable situations as we investigate."

She shivered, thinking of how terrible it would've been if she'd exchanged vows with

Craig. "He wasn't like that when we met." Her gaze drifted toward the warehouse, confirming that Craig remained in cuffs and was surrounded by hard men in black tactical gear. "I don't know when or what made him change."

"Thank you for doing the right thing," Casey said. Turning to Drew, he added, "We have a team searching the bayous for you." He reached for the radio clipped to his belt. "I need to call them back."

"Actually," Drew said, "they should probably pick up Everett's team."

"They were gonna feed us to the gators." Andy's voice held more pride than fear. "But Drew stopped them and then we sank their car."

Addison bit her lip, letting the conversation play out. Her son had earned a few bragging rights after everything they'd survived.

"You look a little wet. Did you fall in?"

"Drew threw me into the swamp so I wasn't in danger."

"I see." Casey arched an eyebrow at Drew. "I'm glad they didn't hurt any of you."

Addison's mind flashed to Drew being tortured with a battery, beaten and shot. She opened her mouth, but Drew put his arm around her. "We all came through."

"We did," Andy agreed. "Mom and Dad—I mean Drew—attacked the bad guys just like

Captain America." He tipped his face to Drew. "Without the shield. I watched it all from a tree. But then I helped sink the car."

Addison lost the rest of the conversation. Andy had called Drew Dad. In her heart the moment felt as big as when he'd taken his first steps or the first time he'd called her Mama. She slid a look at Drew, but his impassive expression gave her no hint to his feelings. He must've heard it. Would it change anything?

"I might just need a statement from you, young man," Casey was saying.

Andy's eyes went wide. "From me?"

"You think you can describe the people you saw?"

"Yes, sir!"

"If it's okay with your mom, we'll step over here and you can tell me everything."

Andy looked up at her hopefully.

"Go on," she said. Apparently Casey's instincts were accurate and he'd noticed she and Drew needed a moment to themselves.

"You were hurt," she began. "Shot and—" she had to swallow "—tortured again. Because of me." The tremor started in her hands as her calm facade cracked apart.

Drew caught her hands and pressed them between his. "You didn't cause any of this. Everett did and he'll pay the penalty."

She leaned close, dropping her forehead to his shoulder, breathing in his warm scent. She could be strong and still be allowed her weak moments. It had always been that way with him. "Thank you."

"For what?"

"For all of it." She forced herself to look up, to meet his warm brown gaze. "I couldn't have saved Andy without you."

"You'd have found a way." His big hands smoothed across her shoulders and down her spine, as if he might simply erase the tension built up there. How could a touch calm and soothe in one moment and ignite a whole new kind of delicious energy in the next? It was just one more of Drew's many talents.

"How long before you head back to San Francisco?"

"I have a few calls to make." First to Professor Hastings and then to her boss to resign. After that, it would be reaching out to Bernadette and Nico's family. Taking a step back, afraid of being hurt by Drew's reaction, she took a big breath and blurted out her decision. "I'm not going back to California. I've decided to stay out here. Andy and I need…" *You*, she thought, but she wouldn't put that kind of pressure on him. "We need a change of pace. I have enough cushion built up until I find work that suits me in this area."

He reached out, winding a curl of her hair around his finger. He'd done that the night they'd met. "You're moving back to the family farm?"

She nodded. "I think Andy will like it out there and any adventures we have will be a thousand times safer."

"It must be pretty run-down."

"No." His face fell and she wished she'd kept the truth to herself, if only so he'd be enticed to help her make a few repairs. "There's a realty service that's kept it up for me."

"Surprised Everett didn't know about it."

She'd never told Craig much about her past. It hadn't felt relevant then, but now she understood it had been a way of keeping Drew's memory safe and treasured. He'd been the gold standard no other man could measure up to.

She was being an idiot here. They both were. "You could come with us. Give yourself a chance to heal up before you head back to whatever is waiting for you in Detroit."

"Is that what you want?"

"Which part?" She wanted the dream that had been snatched from her so many years ago. She wanted family dinners, picnics and baseball games. She wanted movie nights, stargazing and all the joys that came with sharing life's ups and downs with her soul mate. If he wanted that, too.

The words tangled in her throat, so much to say

that she didn't know where to start. She pressed up on her toes, her hands clutching his shoulders for balance as she kissed him, letting him feel everything she wanted.

"I want you to be happy, Drew," she said, breaking the kiss. "This time your happiness has to come first."

His hands rested lightly at her trim waist. Happy? Did he dare take what he thought she was offering? "The day I met you I understood what being happy felt like. It sounds cheesy, but it's true."

She pressed her lips together, her pale blue eyes bright. After everything he thought he knew about her, with all the desperate hope crashing through him, he didn't trust himself to read her reactions correctly. Nothing for it but to barrel on. If he held back now, he'd never shake free of the regret. "I never stopped loving you, Addi. Loving you got me through the darkest days of my life. Give me another chance. Give *us* another chance to have what we once dreamed of. Please."

Her gaze drifted over to where Casey and Andy were talking. "He called you Dad."

"I heard." It wasn't the response to his revelations he'd anticipated, but he wasn't above using Andy as a way in. He wanted to get to know his son and he believed with a little time he could win Addi back, too.

"He's a smart kid." A tear slipped down her cheek and she swiped it away impatiently. "You're the only man I ever wanted him to address that way."

"Does that mean…"

"I never stopped loving what we had, Drew." Her words were tender, but she stepped back again. "I don't think my heart is capable of loving another man like I loved you."

Past tense. Damn it. Sensing the worst, he shoved his hands into his pockets to keep from grabbing her. Every muscle in his body was ready to hold and cling, but he worried that if he made a move before she was ready, he'd scare her away.

"You should know what you're getting into," she said, her eyes on their son.

"Tell me." Good or bad, nothing she could say would sway him from wanting to be part of their lives, however she'd have him. They had a son who wanted and needed his dad and his mom.

"The routine can be monotonous," she began. "School, homework, bedtime."

So far, no problem.

"Moods—"

"Yours or his?"

"Both," she admitted, her lips tilting. "There's soccer and laundry and meals."

"I like to eat," he said, warming to the topic. "I can even cook."

"This is serious."

"I know."

"A commitment."

"I'm ready." He caught the quick hitch of her breath, pressed his advantage. "Whether you can love me again or not, I love our son. Let me be there for him."

"But I want you to be there for *you*." She crossed her arms and glared. "What about your community work in Detroit?"

He shook his head. "Sweetheart, it was a place to hide. Those programs are in good hands, though I wouldn't mind checking in on the kids periodically. I was marking time, that's all, just to keep from interfering in the life you'd created without me."

"There hasn't been a day since we met that you weren't in my life." She tapped her fingers against her heart. "I've been raising Drew 2.0."

"And doing a fine job." He couldn't stand it; he draped an arm around her shoulder. "Let's go the rest of the way together."

"You mean it?"

He nodded. "We have another shot, Addi. Either push me away or tell me you'll marry me so we can get to work on the other three kids we wanted to have."

"You remember that?" she asked on a shaky laugh.

He moved so they were facing each other again. He wouldn't leave room for any doubts. "I remember everything. We wanted four kids and the farmhouse for summer vacations, and by this time I was supposed to be looking for a unit that wouldn't send me away quite so often."

"We were good at the long-distance thing."

"We're better together." He kissed her until they were both breathless. "You were going to teach law once the kids were all in school. On our twenty-fifth anniversary I was going to re-create our honeymoon."

"You thought that far ahead?"

"From the moment you agreed to marry me."

"Where were we going on our honeymoon?"

He had her now, he knew it. "Eight years ago, it was Belize."

"Oh, that sounds nice."

"Now I'm thinking Disneyland."

"Disneyland?"

"It's a family-friendly kind of honeymoon. We'll get a suite," he added with a suggestive wink. "Plus, it puts a positive spin on these major changes in Andy's life and gives him a chance to say goodbye to his friends."

"Don't say that too loudly."

"Why not? Does he hate theme parks?"

"He loves them," she said, gazing up at him. Her mouth curved in her most beautiful smile, her beautiful eyes glowing with happiness. "You'll be an amazing dad."

"I'm crossing my fingers that I'll be half as good as you've been as a mom."

"What if I'm a lousy wife?"

"Not a chance."

"You sound pretty certain. I've been doing the solo act a long time. What if I'm too set in my ways?"

"Not a chance," he repeated. "From where I'm standing you've been making our dreams come true."

"But the most vital piece was missing," she murmured, lacing her fingers with his. "You."

"I'm yours for as long as you'll have me," he said. "I love you, Addison."

"I love you, too. I always will."

"So say you'll marry me and let's start making up for lost time."

"I'll marry you." She wrapped her arms around his neck and pressed her soft body to his. "On one condition."

"Name it."

"Promise me you won't answer any kind of

phone or summons until we exchange vows and you kiss the bride."

He threw his head back and laughed. "It's a deal."

"I might not let you out of my sight between now and then."

"That works just fine for me."

"I can't wait to be your wife."

"We're getting married?" Andy raced over and threw himself into their hug. "You'll be my dad?"

Drew nodded. "I always have been, son."

"Yes!" Andy did a fist pump. "Wait." He stopped his victory dance and stared up at his mom. "Always?"

"It's true," she replied. "Your dad was lost for a long time and no one knew he was even still alive. But he's back now and we're going to be a family."

Drew had never felt more certain about anything when she smiled at him that way. All those wishes on all those stars were finally coming true. "We'll tell you the whole story as soon as we're out of here."

After a brief exchange with Casey, they were cleared to leave, with a protective detail as a final precaution.

Nothing and no one could stop them now.

Epilogue

Addison smoothed a hand over the soft, sleek skirt of her wedding gown, stunned by the absolute lack of butterflies in her stomach. Nerves were expected for any bride, and considering her rocky road to this day, she would've been entitled to plenty. But she knew Drew would be there this time and not just because he sent her a text message update every ten minutes.

She laughed when her phone chimed with another one, this time with a shot of Andy in his tuxedo, practicing serious ring bearer faces in the mirror. She was about to have the happy beginning she'd dreamed of and Andy was about to start a lifetime with his father.

She thought of the farmhouse they would turn into a home after their honeymoon. They would be a family at last. Complete and whole and stronger for the fire that had forged their relationship.

"You made the right choice. Then and now." Bernadette smiled as Addison checked her reflection one last time.

"I did." She'd gone back and forth about the dress. Drew hadn't seen the original, and during the whirlwind planning for today, he'd carefully avoided any reference to their first wedding attempt. She and Bernadette had shopped boutiques and she'd tried on gowns in various styles, but nothing else felt as right as the gown she'd chosen the first time.

With her mother's pearls glowing above the strapless sweetheart neckline and the lace that hugged her curves from bust to waist, she hoped to make Drew's jaw drop. But she hadn't done a complete carbon copy of the day he'd missed. That wouldn't honor what they'd been through. Instead of an updo with a veil, she left her hair down in loose waves, pulled back from her face with luminous pearl-studded combs.

"Take your bouquet and let's go or Drew will think you've left him this time."

She laughed. "Never!" As she waited out of sight for Andy and then Bernadette to enter the small chapel, she sighed happily.

"Ready?" Professor Hastings offered his arm.

"More than." She beamed. "Here's to the first moment of the best days of our lives."

"You look lovely," he whispered, making her smile as the music changed for her procession.

She felt lovely. She'd felt confident and beautiful in the dressing room, but when Drew's eyes locked with hers the awareness shifted to an all-new high. With him in his tuxedo, with their son by his side, her world felt complete at last. It was a priceless image she'd hold in her heart forever.

Her steps were sure, her smile unquenchable as she approached the altar. At last she and Drew could seize the dream that had been stolen from them eight years ago. The words and motions of the ceremony barely registered, her heart was so full of Drew and the sheer joy between them.

With the exchange of vows and rings, she heard the words that mattered most, the words she so recently thought would never be spoken for her— "I now pronounce you husband and wife. You may kiss the bride."

Drew's lips were warm and gentle and a loud cheer nearly blew the roof off the chapel when they turned to face everyone who'd come to celebrate their wedding.

Her arm linked with Drew's, she felt as if she were floating on a cloud down the aisle.

"Happy?" Drew asked as he helped her into the carriage that would take them to the reception.

"That's not a big enough word for everything I feel, but it's a good start." She looked at him, seeing the happiness and love in his eyes. "You can't be worried I'll have regrets."

"I'm not." He gave her hand a squeeze, rubbing his thumb over the gleaming gold of her wedding band. "It's hard to believe this day is real. It's a miracle."

"Yes, it is."

"But we're not the same people we were when we first attempted this," he said.

She patted his thigh, so grateful she'd have the rest of her life to share affection and passion in equal measure. "Allow me to disagree. We've both had some hard mileage in the years we were apart, but it made us stronger individuals. Nothing we've been through changed my soul-deep love for you."

"I love you, Mrs. Bryant."

Sweeter words were never spoken. His sexy grin made her pulse jump. She tipped her face up for a lingering, searing kiss this time. "I love you, too, Mr. Bryant. It will only ever be you for me."

"HE'D MAKE ONE hell of a Specialist," Emmett said quietly to Thomas as Drew and Addison mingled with their guests at the reception. "If not in the field, as an instructor."

"I offered," Thomas said as the happy couple

moved out in front of the band for their first dance as husband and wife. "He turned me down."

"Our loss."

"Yes, but I sure don't hold his priorities against him." Thomas slid a look across the table where his wife was chatting with his sister and Emmett's wife, Cecelia. How much longer before he and Jo could get started on their own family? "Drew and Addison have done more than enough for their country. They need some space to make up for lost time."

As if on cue, Andy rushed onto the dance floor and Drew scooped him up. The three of them swayed to the music and hope radiated like sunshine from the young family.

Emmett escorted Cecelia out when the music changed and Thomas walked over, extending a hand to Jo. The happiness was contagious, he thought. With his wife in his arms, and the romance swirling around them, he pushed away thoughts of work, enjoying the hard-earned peace of the present moment.

Tomorrow was soon enough to think about the next assignment.

* * * * *